An American Christmas Treasury

A Collection of Classic Holiday Stories of Joy, Magic, and Tradition

Intanjible Publishing

Contents

Introduction

Christmas has always been more than a date on the calendar. It's a season of stories. Throughout America's history, some of its finest authors have turned their pens toward the holiday, weaving tales that capture the warmth of the hearth, the sparkle of snow on a moonlit street, and the enduring power of kindness. In these pages, you will find a selection of such works, written during a time when storytelling was both entertainment and a shared tradition. They remind us that while fashions and technologies may change, the themes of generosity, hope, and togetherness are timeless.

This collection brings together classic American Christmas tales that span the sentimental, the humorous, and the magical. You'll encounter bustling towns wrapped in garlands, quiet farmhouses lit by a single candle, and characters whose small acts of love make all the difference. Some stories may be familiar friends you've met before; others may be delightful discoveries, waiting to take their place among your holiday favorites.

When curating these dozen tales, I deliberately selected authors known for the fantastical (L. Frank Baum), the traditional (Louisa May Alcott), the impactful (O. Henry), and all stops in between. In total, the works of ten writers are showcased herein. Together, they offer a portrait of Christmas as it has been cherished in America for over a century.

Raywat Deonandan, Editor.

The Gift of the Magi

by O. Henry (1905)

One dollar and eighty-seven cents. That was all. And sixty cents of it was in pennies. Pennies saved one and two at a time by bulldozing the grocer and the vegetable man and the butcher until one's cheeks burned with the silent imputation of parsimony that such close dealing implied. Three times Della counted it. One dollar and eighty-seven cents. And the next day would be Christmas.

There was clearly nothing to do but flop down on the shabby little couch and howl. So Della did it. Which instigates the moral reflection that life is made up of sobs, sniffles, and smiles, with sniffles predominating.

While the mistress of the home is gradually subsiding from the first stage to the second, take a look at the home. A furnished flat at $8 per week. It did not exactly beggar description, but it certainly had that word on the lookout for the mendicancy squad.

In the vestibule below was a letter-box into which no letter would go, and an electric button from which no mortal finger could coax a ring. Also appertaining thereunto was a card bearing the name "Mr. James Dillingham Young."

The "Dillingham" had been flung to the breeze during a former period of prosperity when its possessor was being paid $30 per week. Now, when the income was shrunk to $20, though, they were thinking seriously of contracting to a modest and unassuming D. But whenever Mr. James Dillingham Young came home and reached his flat above he was called "Jim" and greatly hugged by Mrs. James Dillingham Young, already introduced to you as Della. Which is all very good.

Della finished her cry and attended to her cheeks with the powder rag. She stood by the window and looked out dully at a gray cat walking a gray fence in a gray backyard. Tomorrow would be Christmas Day, and she had only $1.87 with which to buy Jim a present. She had been saving every penny she could for months, with this result. Twenty dollars a week doesn't go far. Expenses had been greater than she had calculated. They always are. Only $1.87 to buy a present for Jim. Her Jim. Many a happy hour she had spent planning for something nice for him. Something fine and rare and sterling—something just a little bit near to being worthy of the honor of being owned by Jim.

There was a pier glass between the windows of the room. Perhaps you have seen a pier glass in an $8 flat. A very thin and very agile person may, by observing his reflection in a rapid sequence of longitudinal strips, obtain a fairly accurate conception of his looks. Della, being slender, had mastered the art.

Suddenly she whirled from the window and stood before the glass. Her eyes were shining brilliantly, but her face had lost its color within twenty seconds. Rapidly she pulled down her hair and let it fall to its full length.

Now, there were two possessions of the James Dillingham Youngs in which they both took a mighty pride. One was Jim's gold watch that had been his father's and his grandfather's. The other was Della's hair. Had the queen of Sheba lived in the flat across the airshaft, Della would have let her hair hang out the window some day to dry just to depreciate Her Majesty's jewels and gifts. Had King Solomon been the janitor, with all his treasures piled up in the basement, Jim would have pulled out his watch every time he passed, just to see him pluck at his beard from envy.

So now Della's beautiful hair fell about her rippling and shining like a cascade of brown waters. It reached below her knee and made itself almost a garment for her. And then she did it up again nervously and quickly. Once she faltered for a minute and stood still while a tear or two splashed on the worn red carpet.

On went her old brown jacket; on went her old brown hat. With a whirl of skirts and with the brilliant sparkle still in her eyes, she fluttered out the door and down the stairs to the street.

Where she stopped the sign read: "Mme. Sofronie. Hair Goods of All Kinds." One flight up Della ran, and collected herself, panting. Madame, large, too white, chilly, hardly looked the "Sofronie."

"Will you buy my hair?" asked Della.

"I buy hair," said Madame. "Take yer hat off and let's have a sight at the looks of it."

Down rippled the brown cascade.

"Twenty dollars," said Madame, lifting the mass with a practised hand.

"Give it to me quick," said Della.

Oh, and the next two hours tripped by on rosy wings. Forget the hashed metaphor. She was ransacking the stores for Jim's present.

She found it at last. It surely had been made for Jim and no one else. There was no other like it in any of the stores, and she had turned all of them inside out. It was a platinum fob chain simple and chaste in design, properly proclaiming its value by substance alone and not by meretricious ornamentation—as all good things should do. It was even worthy of The Watch. As soon as she saw it she knew that it must be Jim's. It was like him. Quietness and value—the description applied to both. Twenty-one dollars they took from her for it, and she hurried home with the 87 cents. With that chain on his watch Jim might be properly anxious about the time in any company. Grand as the watch was, he sometimes looked at it on the sly on account of the old leather strap that he used in place of a chain.

When Della reached home her intoxication gave way a little to prudence and reason. She got out her curling irons and lighted the gas and went to work repairing the ravages made by generosity added to love. Which is always a tremendous task, dear friends—a mammoth task.

Within forty minutes her head was covered with tiny, close-lying curls that made her look wonderfully like a truant schoolboy. She looked at her reflection in the mirror long, carefully, and critically.

"If Jim doesn't kill me," she said to herself, "before he takes a second look at me, he'll say I look like a Coney Island chorus girl. But what could I do—oh! what could I do with a dollar and eighty-seven cents?"

At 7 o'clock the coffee was made and the frying-pan was on the back of the stove hot and ready to cook the chops.

Jim was never late. Della doubled the fob chain in her hand and sat on the corner of the table near the door that he always entered. Then she heard his step on the stair away down on the first flight, and she turned white for just a moment. She had a habit of saying a little silent prayer about the simplest everyday things, and now she whispered: "Please God, make him think I am still pretty."

The door opened and Jim stepped in and closed it. He looked thin and very serious. Poor fellow, he was only twenty-two—and to be burdened with a family! He needed a new overcoat and he was without gloves.

Jim stopped inside the door, as immovable as a setter at the scent of quail. His eyes were fixed upon Della, and there was an expression in them that she could not read, and it terrified her. It was not anger, nor surprise, nor disapproval, nor horror, nor any of the sentiments that she had been prepared for. He simply stared at her fixedly with that peculiar expression on his face.

Della wriggled off the table and went for him.

"Jim, darling," she cried, "don't look at me that way. I had my hair cut off and sold because I couldn't have lived through Christmas without giving you a present. It'll grow out again—you won't mind, will you? I just had to do it. My hair grows awfully fast. Say 'Merry Christmas!' Jim, and let's be happy. You don't know what a nice—what a beautiful, nice gift I've got for you."

"You've cut off your hair?" asked Jim, laboriously, as if he had not arrived at that patent fact yet even after the hardest mental labor.

"Cut it off and sold it," said Della. "Don't you like me just as well, anyhow? I'm me without my hair, ain't I?"

Jim looked about the room curiously.

"You say your hair is gone?" he said, with an air almost of idiocy.

"You needn't look for it," said Della. "It's sold, I tell you—sold and gone, too. It's Christmas Eve, boy. Be good to me, for it went for you. Maybe the hairs of my head were numbered," she went on with sudden serious sweetness, "but nobody could ever count my love for you. Shall I put the chops on, Jim?"

Out of his trance Jim seemed quickly to wake. He enfolded his Della. For ten seconds let us regard with discreet scrutiny some inconsequential object in the other direction. Eight dollars a week or a million a year—what is the difference? A mathematician or a wit would give you the wrong answer. The magi brought valuable gifts, but that was not among them. This dark assertion will be illuminated later on.

Jim drew a package from his overcoat pocket and threw it upon the table.

"Don't make any mistake, Dell," he said, "about me. I don't think there's anything in the way of a haircut or a shave or a shampoo that could make me like my girl any less. But if you'll unwrap that package you may see why you had me going a while at first."

White fingers and nimble tore at the string and paper. And then an ecstatic scream of joy; and then, alas! a quick feminine change to hysterical tears and wails, necessitating the immediate employment of all the comforting powers of the lord of the flat.

For there lay The Combs—the set of combs, side and back, that Della had worshipped long in a Broadway window. Beautiful combs, pure tortoise shell, with jewelled rims—just the shade to wear in the beautiful vanished hair. They were expensive combs, she knew, and her heart had simply craved and yearned over them without the least hope of possession. And now, they were hers, but the tresses that should have adorned the coveted adornments were gone.

But she hugged them to her bosom, and at length she was able to look up with dim eyes and a smile and say: "My hair grows so fast, Jim!"

And then Della leaped up like a little singed cat and cried, "Oh, oh!"

Jim had not yet seen his beautiful present. She held it out to him eagerly upon her open palm. The dull precious metal seemed to flash with a reflection of her bright and ardent spirit.

"Isn't it a dandy, Jim? I hunted all over town to find it. You'll have to look at the time a hundred times a day now. Give me your watch. I want to see how it looks on it."

Instead of obeying, Jim tumbled down on the couch and put his hands under the back of his head and smiled.

"Dell," said he, "let's put our Christmas presents away and keep 'em a while. They're too nice to use just at present. I sold the watch to get the money to buy your combs. And now suppose you put the chops on."

The magi, as you know, were wise men—wonderfully wise men—who brought gifts to the Babe in the manger. They invented the art of giving Christmas presents. Being wise, their gifts were no doubt wise ones, possibly bearing the privilege of exchange in case of duplication. And here I have lamely related to you the uneventful chronicle of two foolish children in a flat who most unwisely sacrificed for each other the greatest treasures of their house. But in a last word to the wise of these days let it be said that of all who give gifts these two were the wisest. Of all who give and receive gifts, such as they are wisest. Everywhere they are wisest. They are the magi.

A Visit from St. Nicholas

by Clement Clarke Moore (1823)

'Twas the night before Christmas, when all through the house

Not a creature was stirring, not even a mouse;

The stockings were hung by the chimney with care,

In hopes that St. Nicholas soon would be there;

The children were nestled all snug in their beds;

While visions of sugar-plums danced in their heads;

And mamma in her 'kerchief, and I in my cap,

Had just settled our brains for a long winter's nap,

When out on the lawn there arose such a clatter,

I sprang from my bed to see what was the matter.

Away to the window I flew like a flash,

Tore open the shutters and threw up the sash.

The moon on the breast of the new-fallen snow,

Gave a lustre of midday to objects below,

When what to my wondering eyes did appear,

But a miniature sleigh and eight tiny rein-deer,

With a little old driver so lively and quick,

I knew in a moment he must be St. Nick.

More rapid than eagles his coursers they came,

And he whistled, and shouted, and called them by name:

"Now, Dasher! now, Dancer! now Prancer and Vixen!

On, Comet! on, Cupid! on, Donder and Blitzen!

To the top of the porch! to the top of the wall!

Now dash away! dash away! dash away all!"

As leaves that before the wild hurricane fly,

When they meet with an obstacle, mount to the sky;

So up to the housetop the coursers they flew

With the sleigh full of toys, and St. Nicholas too—

And then, in a twinkling, I heard on the roof

The prancing and pawing of each little hoof.

As I drew in my head, and was turning around,

Down the chimney St. Nicholas came with a bound.
He was dressed all in fur, from his head to his foot,
And his clothes were all tarnished with ashes and soot;
A bundle of toys he had flung on his back,
And he looked like a pedler just opening his pack.
His eyes—how they twinkled! his dimples, how merry!
His cheeks were like roses, his nose like a cherry!
His droll little mouth was drawn up like a bow,
And the beard on his chin was as white as the snow;
The stump of a pipe he held tight in his teeth,
And the smoke, it encircled his head like a wreath;
He had a broad face and a little round belly
That shook when he laughed, like a bowl full of jelly.
He was chubby and plump, a right jolly old elf,
And I laughed when I saw him, in spite of myself;
A wink of his eye and a twist of his head
Soon gave me to know I had nothing to dread;
He spoke not a word, but went straight to his work,
And filled all the stockings; then turned with a jerk,
And laying his finger aside of his nose,

And giving a nod, up the chimney he rose;

He sprang to his sleigh, to his team gave a whistle,

And away they all flew like the down of a thistle.

But I heard him exclaim, ere he drove out of sight—

"Happy Christmas to all, and to all a good night!"

Little Gretchen and the Wooden Shoe

by Elizabeth Harrison (1891)

Once upon a time - so long ago that everybody has forgotten the date - in a city in the north of Europe - with such a hard name that nobody can ever remember it - there was a little seven-year-old boy named Wolff, whose parents were dead, who lived with a cross and stingy old aunt, who never thought of kissing him more than once a year and who sighed deeply whenever she gave him a bowlful of soup.

But the poor little fellow had such a sweet nature that in spite of everything, he loved the old woman, although he was terribly afraid of her and could never look at her ugly old face without shivering.

As this aunt of little Wolff was known to have a house of her own and an old woollen stocking full of gold, she had not dared to send the boy to a charity school; but, in order to get a reduction in the price, she had so wrangled with the master of the school, to which little Wolff finally went, that this bad man, vexed at having a pupil so poorly dressed and paying so little, often punished him unjustly, and even prejudiced his companions against him, so that the three boys, all sons of rich parents, made a drudge and laughing stock of the little fellow.

The poor little one was thus as wretched as a child could be and used to hide himself in corners to weep whenever Christmas time came.

It was the schoolmaster's custom to take all his pupils to the midnight mass on Christmas Eve, and to bring them home again afterward.

Now, as the winter this year was very bitter, and as heavy snow had been falling for several days, all the boys came well bundled up in warm clothes, with fur caps pulled over their ears, padded jackets, gloves and knitted mittens, and strong, thick-soled boots. Only little Wolff presented himself shivering in the poor clothes he used to wear both weekdays and Sundays and having on his feet only thin socks in heavy wooden shoes.

His naughty companions noticing his sad face and awkward appearance, made many jokes at his expense; but the little fellow was so busy blowing on his fingers, and was suffering so much with chilblains, that he took no notice of them. So the band of youngsters, walking two and two behind the master, started for the church.

It was pleasant in the church which was brilliant with lighted candles; and the boys excited by the warmth took advantage of the music of the choir and the organ to chatter among themselves in low tones. They bragged about the fun that was awaiting them at home. The mayor's son had seen, just before starting off, an immense goose ready stuffed and dressed for cooking. At the alderman's home there was a little pine-tree with branches laden down with oranges, sweets, and toys. And the lawyer's cook had put on her cap with such care as she never thought of taking unless she was expecting something very good!

Then they talked, too, of all that the Christ-Child was going to bring them, of all he was going to put in their shoes which, you might be sure, they would take good care to leave in the chimney place before going to bed; and the eyes of these little urchins, as lively as a cage of mice, were sparkling in advance over the joy they would have when they awoke in the morning and saw the pink bag full of sugar-plums, the little lead soldiers ranged in companies in their boxes, the menageries smelling of varnished wood, and the magnificent jumping-jacks in purple and tinsel.

Alas! Little Wolff knew by experience that his old miser of an aunt would send him to bed supperless, but, with childlike faith and certain of having been, all the year, as good and industrious as possible, he hoped that the Christ-Child would not forget him, and so he, too, planned to place his wooden shoes in good time in the fireplace.

Midnight mass over, the worshippers departed, eager for their fun, and the band of pupils always walking two and two, and following the teacher, left the church.

Now, in the porch and seated on a stone bench set in the niche of a painted arch, a child was sleeping - a child in a white woollen garment, but with his little feet bare, in spite of the cold. He was not a beggar, for his garment was white and new, and near him on the floor was a bundle of carpenter's tools.

In the clear light of the stars, his face, with its closed eyes, shone with an expression of divine sweetness, and his long, curling, blond locks seemed to form a halo about his brow. But his little child's feet, made blue by the cold of this bitter December night, were pitiful to see!

The boys so well clothed for the winter weather passed by quite indifferent to the unknown child; several of them, sons of the notables of the town, however, cast on the vagabond looks in which could be read all the scorn of the rich for the poor, of the well-fed for the hungry.

But little Wolff, coming last out of the church, stopped, deeply touched, before the beautiful sleeping child.

"Oh, dear!" said the little fellow to himself, "this is frightful! This poor little one has no shoes and stockings in this bad weather - and, what is still worse, he has not even a wooden shoe to leave near him to-night while he sleeps, into which the little Christ-Child can put something good to soothe his misery."

And carried away by his loving heart, Wolff drew the wooden shoe from his right foot, laid it down before the sleeping child, and, as best he could, sometimes hopping, sometimes limping with his sock wet by the snow, he went home to his aunt.

"Look at the good-for-nothing!" cried the old woman, full of wrath at the sight of the shoeless boy. "What have you done with your shoe, you little villain?"

Little Wolff did not know how to lie, so, although trembling with terror when he saw the rage of the old shrew, he tried to relate his adventure.

But the miserly old creature only burst into a frightful fit of laughter.

"Aha! So my young gentleman strips himself for the beggars. Aha! My young gentleman breaks his pair of shoes for a bare-foot! Here is something new, forsooth. Very well, since it is this way, I shall put the only shoe that is left into the chimney-place, and I'll answer for it that the Christ-Child will put in something to-night to beat you with in the morning! And you will have only a crust of bread and water to-morrow. And we shall see if the next time, you will be giving your shoes to the first vagabond that happens along."

And the wicked woman having boxed the ears of the poor little fellow, made him climb up into the loft where he had his wretched cubbyhole.

Desolate, the child went to bed in the dark and soon fell asleep, but his pillow was wet with tears.

But behold! the next morning when the old woman, awakened early by the cold, went downstairs - oh, wonder of wonders - she saw the big chimney filled with shining toys, bags of magnificent bonbons, and riches of every sort, and standing out in front of all this treasure, was the right wooden shoe which the boy had given to the little vagabond, yes, and beside it, the one which she had placed in the chimney to hold the bunch of switches.

As little Wolff, attracted by the cries of his aunt, stood in an ecstasy of childish delight before the splendid Christmas gifts, shouts of laughter were heard outside. The woman and child ran out to see what all this meant, and behold! all the gossips of the town were standing around the public fountain. What could have happened? Oh, a most ridiculous and extraordinary thing! The children of the richest men in the town, whom their parents had planned to surprise with the most beautiful presents had found only switches in their shoes!

Then the old woman and the child thinking of all the riches in their chimney were filled with fear. But suddenly they saw the priest appear, his countenance full of astonishment. Just above the bench placed near the door of the church, in the very spot where, the night before, a child in a white garment and with bare feet, in spite of the cold, had rested his lovely head, the priest had found a circlet of gold imbedded in the old stones.

Then, they all crossed themselves devoutly, perceiving that this beautiful sleeping child with the carpenter's tools had been Jesus of Nazareth himself, who had come back for one hour just as he had been when he used to work in the home of his parents; and reverently they bowed before this miracle, which the good God had done to reward the faith and the love of a little child.

Beasley's Christmas Party

by Booth Tarkington (1909)

I

The maple-bordered street was as still as a country Sunday; so quiet that there seemed an echo to my footsteps. It was four o'clock in the morning; clear October moonlight misted through the thinning foliage to the shadowy sidewalk and lay like a transparent silver fog upon the house of my admiration, as I strode along, returning from my first night's work on the "Wainwright Morning Despatch."

I had already marked that house as the finest (to my taste) in Wainwright, though hitherto, on my excursions to this metropolis, the state capital, I was not without a certain native jealousy that Spencerville, the county-seat where I lived, had nothing so good. Now, however, I approached its purlieus with a pleasure in it quite unalloyed, for I was at last myself a resident (albeit of only one day's standing) of Wainwright, and the house—though I had not even an idea who lived there—part of my possessions as a citizen. Moreover, I might enjoy the warmer pride of a next-door-neighbor, for Mrs. Apperthwaite's, where I had taken a room, was just beyond.

This was the quietest part of Wainwright; business stopped short of it, and the "fashionable residence section" had overleaped this "forgotten backwater," leaving it undisturbed and unchanging, with that look about it which is the quality of few urban quarters, and eventually of none, as a town grows to be a city—the look of still being a neighborhood. This friendliness of appearance was largely the emanation of the homely and beautiful house which so greatly pleased my fancy.

It might be difficult to say why I thought it the "finest" house in Wainwright, for a simpler structure would be hard to imagine; it was merely a big, old-fashioned brick house, painted brown and very plain, set well away from the street among some splendid forest trees, with a fair spread of flat lawn. But it gave back a great deal for your glance, just as some people do. It was a large house, as I say, yet it looked not like a mansion but like a home; and made you wish that you lived in it. Or, driving by, of an evening, you would have liked to hitch your horse and go in; it spoke so surely of hearty, old-fashioned people living there, who would welcome you merrily.

It looked like a house where there were a grandfather and a grandmother; where holidays were warmly kept; where there were boisterous family reunions to which uncles and aunts, who had been born there, would return from no matter what distances; a house where big turkeys would be on the table often; where one called "the hired man" (and named either Abner or Ole) would crack walnuts upon a flat-iron clutched between his knees on the back porch; it looked like a house where they played charades; where there would be long streamers of evergreen and dozens of wreaths of holly at Christmas-time; where there were tearful, happy weddings and great throwings of rice after little brides, from the broad front steps: in a word, it was the sort of a house to make the hearts of spinsters and bachelors very lonely and wistful—and that is about as near as I can come to my reason for thinking it the finest house in Wainwright.

The moon hung kindly above its level roof in the silence of that October morning, as I checked my gait to loiter along the picket fence; but suddenly the house showed a light of its own. The spurt of a match took my eye to one of the upper windows, then a steadier glow of orange told me that a lamp was lighted. The window was opened, and a man looked out and whistled loudly.

I stopped, thinking that he meant to attract my attention; that something might be wrong; that perhaps some one was needed to go for a doctor. My mistake was immediately evident, however; I stood in the shadow of the trees bordering the sidewalk, and the man at the window had not seen me.

"Boy! Boy!" he called, softly. "Where are you, Simpledoria?"

He leaned from the window, looking downward. "Why, THERE you are!" he exclaimed, and turned to address some invisible person within the room. "He's right there, underneath the window. I'll bring him up." He leaned out again. "Wait there, Simpledoria!" he called. "I'll be down in a jiffy and let you in."

Puzzled, I stared at the vacant lawn before me. The clear moonlight revealed it brightly, and it was empty of any living presence; there were no bushes nor shrubberies—nor even shadows—that could have been mistaken for a boy, if

"Simpledoria" WAS a boy. There was no dog in sight; there was no cat; there was nothing beneath the window except thick, close-cropped grass.

A light shone in the hallway behind the broad front doors; one of these was opened, and revealed in silhouette the tall, thin figure of a man in a long, old-fashioned dressing-gown.

"Simpledoria," he said, addressing the night air with considerable severity, "I don't know what to make of you. You might have caught your death of cold, roving out at such an hour. But there," he continued, more indulgently; "wipe your feet on the mat and come in. You're safe NOW!"

He closed the door, and I heard him call to some one up-stairs, as he rearranged the fastenings:

"Simpledoria is all right—only a little chilled. I'll bring him up to your fire."

I went on my way in a condition of astonishment that engendered, almost, a doubt of my eyes; for if my sight was unimpaired and myself not subject to optical or mental delusion, neither boy nor dog nor bird nor cat, nor any other object of this visible world, had entered that opened door. Was my "finest" house, then, a place of call for wandering ghosts, who came home to roost at four in the morning?

It was only a step to Mrs. Apperthwaite's; I let myself in with the key that good lady had given me, stole up to my room, went to my window, and stared across the yard at the house next door. The front window in the second story, I decided, necessarily belonged to that room in which the lamp had been lighted; but all was dark there now. I went to bed, and dreamed that I was out at sea in a fog, having embarked on a transparent vessel whose preposterous name, inscribed upon glass life-belts, depending here and there from an invisible rail, was SIMPLEDORIA.

II

Mrs. Apperthwaite's was a commodious old house, the greater part of it of about the same age, I judged, as its neighbor; but the late Mr. Apperthwaite had caught the Mansard fever of the late 'Seventies, and the building-disease, once fastened upon him, had never known a convalescence, but, rather, a series of relapses, the tokens of which, in the nature of a cupola and a couple of frame turrets, were terrifyingly apparent. These romantic misplacements seemed to me not inharmonious with the library, a cheerful and pleasantly shabby apartment down-stairs, where I found (over a substratum of history, encyclopaedia, and family Bible) some worn old volumes of Godey's Lady's Book, an early edition of Cooper's works; Scott, Bulwer, Macaulay, Byron, and Tennyson, complete; some odd volumes of Victor Hugo, of the elder Dumas, of Flaubert, of Gautier, and of Balzac; Clarissa, Lalla Rookh, The Alhambra, Beulah, Uarda, Lucile, Uncle Tom's Cabin, Ben-Hur, Trilby, She, Little Lord Fauntleroy; and of a later decade, there were novels about those delicately tangled emotions experienced by the supreme few; and stories of adventurous royalty; tales of "clean-limbed young American manhood;" and some thin volumes of rather precious verse.

'Twas amid these romantic scenes that I awaited the sound of the lunch-bell (which for me was the announcement of breakfast), when I arose from my first night's slumbers under Mrs. Apperthwaite's roof; and I wondered if the books were a fair mirror of Miss Apperthwaite's mind (I had been told that Mrs. Apperthwaite had a daughter). Mrs. Apperthwaite herself, in her youth, might have sat to an illustrator of Scott or Bulwer. Even now you could see she had come as near being romantically beautiful as was consistently proper for such a timid, gentle little gentlewoman as she was. Reduced, by her husband's insolvency (coincident with his demise) to "keeping boarders," she did it gracefully, as if the urgency thereto were only a spirit of quiet hospitality. It should be added in haste that she set an excellent table.

Moreover, the guests who gathered at her board were of a very attractive description, as I decided the instant my eye fell upon the lady who sat opposite me at lunch. I knew at once that she was Miss Apperthwaite, she "went so," as they say, with her mother; nothing could have been more suitable. Mrs. Apperthwaite was the kind of woman whom you would expect to have a beautiful daughter, and Miss Apperthwaite more than fulfilled her mother's promise.

I guessed her to be more than Juliet Capulet's age, indeed, yet still between that and the perfect age of woman. She was of a larger, fuller, more striking type than Mrs. Apperthwaite, a bolder type, one might put it—though she might have been a great deal bolder than Mrs. Apperthwaite without being bold. Certainly she was handsome enough to make it difficult for a young fellow to keep from staring at her. She had an abundance of very soft, dark hair, worn almost severely, as if its profusion necessitated repression; and I am compelled to admit that her fine eyes expressed a distant contemplation—obviously of habit not of mood—so pronounced that one of her enemies (if she had any) might have described them as "dreamy."

Only one other of my own sex was present at the lunch-table, a Mr. Dowden, an elderly lawyer and politician of whom I had heard, and to whom Mrs. Apperthwaite, coming in after the rest of us were seated, introduced me. She made the presentation general; and I had the experience of receiving a nod and a slow glance, in which there was a sort of dusky, estimating brilliance, from the beautiful lady opposite me.

It might have been better mannered for me to address myself to Mr. Dowden, or one of the very nice elderly women, who were my fellow-guests, than to open a conversation with Miss Apperthwaite; but I did not stop to think of that.

“You have a splendid old house next door to you here, Miss Apperthwaite,” I said. “It's a privilege to find it in view from my window.”

There was a faint stir as of some consternation in the little company. The elderly ladies stopped talking abruptly and exchanged glances, though this was not of my observation at the moment, I think, but recurred to my consciousness later, when I had perceived my blunder.

“May I ask who lives there?” I pursued.

Miss Apperthwaite allowed her noticeable lashes to cover her eyes for an instant, then looked up again.

“A Mr. Beasley,” she said.

“Not the Honorable David Beasley!” I exclaimed.

“Yes,” she returned, with a certain gravity which I afterward wished had checked me. “Do you know him?”

"Not in person," I explained. "You see, I've written a good deal about him. I was with the "Spencerville Journal" until a few days ago, and even in the country we know who's who in politics over the state. Beasley's the man that went to Congress and never made a speech—never made even a motion to adjourn—but got everything his district wanted. There's talk of him now for Governor."

"Indeed?"

"And so it's the Honorable David Beasley who lives in that splendid place. How curious that is!"

"Why?" asked Miss Apperthwaite.

"It seems too big for one man," I answered; "and I've always had the impression Mr. Beasley was a bachelor."

"Yes," she said, rather slowly, "he is."

"But of course he doesn't live there all alone," I supposed, aloud, "probably he has—"

"No. There's no one else—except a couple of colored servants."

"What a crime!" I exclaimed. "If there ever was a house meant for a large family, that one is. Can't you almost hear it crying out for heaps and heaps of romping children? I should think—"

I was interrupted by a loud cough from Mr. Dowden, so abrupt and artificial that his intention to check the flow of my innocent prattle was embarrassingly obvious—even to me!

"Can you tell me," he said, leaning forward and following up the interruption as hastily as possible, "what the farmers were getting for their wheat when you left Spencerville?"

"Ninety-four cents," I answered, and felt my ears growing red with mortification. Too late, I remembered that the new-comer in a community should guard his tongue among the natives until he has unravelled the skein of their relationships, alliances, feuds, and private wars—a precept not unlike the classic injunction:

"Yes, my darling daughter. Hang your clothes on a hickory limb, But don't go near the water."

However, in my confusion I warmly regretted my failure to follow it, and resolved not to blunder again.

Mr. Dowden thanked me for the information for which he had no real desire, and, the elderly ladies again taking up (with all too evident relief) their various mild debates, he inquired if I played bridge. "But I forget," he added. "Of course you'll be at the 'Despatch' office in the evenings, and can't be here." After which he immediately began to question me about my work, making his determination to give me no opportunity again to mention the Honorable David Beasley unnecessarily conspicuous, as I thought.

I could only conclude that some unpleasantness had arisen between himself and Beasley, probably of political origin, since they were both in politics, and of personal (and consequently bitter) development; and that Mr. Dowden found the mention of Beasley not only unpleasant to himself but a possible embarrassment to the ladies (who, I supposed, were aware of the quarrel) on his account.

After lunch, not having to report at the office immediately, I took unto myself the solace of a cigar, which kept me company during a stroll about Mrs. Apperthwaite's capacious yard. In the rear I found an old-fashioned rose-garden—the bushes long since bloomless and now brown with autumn—and I paced its gravelled paths up and down, at the same time favoring Mr. Beasley's house with a covert study that would have done credit to a porch-climber, for the sting of my blunder at the table was quiescent, or at least neutralized, under the itch of a curiosity far from satisfied concerning the interesting premises next door. The gentleman in the dressing-gown, I was sure, could have been no other than the Honorable David Beasley himself. He came not in eyeshot now, neither he nor any other; there was no sign of life about the place. That portion of his yard which lay behind the house was not within my vision, it is true, his property being here separated from Mrs. Apperthwaite's by a board fence higher than a tall man could reach; but there was no sound from the other side of this partition, save that caused by the quiet movement of rusty leaves in the breeze.

My cigar was at half-length when the green lattice door of Mrs. Apperthwaite's back porch was opened and Miss Apperthwaite, bearing a saucer of milk, issued therefrom, followed, hastily, by a very white, fat cat, with a pink ribbon round its neck, a vibrant nose, and fixed, voracious eyes uplifted to the saucer. The lady and her cat offered to view a group as pretty as a popular painting; it was even improved when, stooping, Miss Apperthwaite set the saucer upon the ground, and, continuing in that posture, stroked the cat. To bend so far is a test of a woman's grace, I have observed.

She turned her face toward me and smiled. "I'm almost at the age, you see."

"What age?" I asked, stupidly enough.

"When we take to cats," she said, rising. "Spinsterhood" we like to call it. 'Single-blessedness!'"

"That is your kind heart. You decline to make one of us happy to the despair of all the rest."

She laughed at this, though with no very genuine mirth, I marked, and let my 1830 attempt at gallantry pass without other retort.

"You seemed interested in the old place yonder." She indicated Mr. Beasley's house with a nod.

"Oh, I understood my blunder," I said, quickly. "I wish I had known the subject was embarrassing or unpleasant to Mr. Dowden."

"What made you think that?"

"Surely," I said, "you saw how pointedly he cut me off."

"Yes," she returned, thoughtfully. "He rather did; it's true. At least, I see how you got that impression." She seemed to muse upon this, letting her eyes fall; then, raising them, allowed her far-away gaze to rest upon the house beyond the fence, and said, "It IS an interesting old place."

"And Mr. Beasley himself—" I began.

"Oh," she said, "HE isn't interesting. That's his trouble!"

"You mean his trouble not to—"

She interrupted me, speaking with sudden, surprising energy, "I mean he's a man of no imagination."

"No imagination!" I exclaimed.

“None in the world! Not one ounce of imagination! Not one grain!”

“Then who,” I cried—“or what—is Simpledoria?”

“Simple—what?” she said, plainly mystified.

“Simpledoria.”

“Simpledoria?” she repeated, and laughed. “What in the world is that?”

“You never heard of it before?”

“Never in my life.”

“You've lived next door to Mr. Beasley a long time, haven't you?”

“All my life.”

“And I suppose you must know him pretty well.”

“What next?” she said, smiling.

“You said he lived there all alone,” I went on, tentatively.

“Except for an old colored couple, his servants.”

“Can you tell me—” I hesitated. “Has he ever been thought—well, 'queer'?”

“Never!” she answered, emphatically. “Never anything so exciting! Merely deadly and hopelessly commonplace.” She picked up the saucer, now exceedingly empty, and set it upon a shelf by the lattice door. “What was it about—what was that name?—'Simpledoria'?”

"I will tell you," I said. And I related in detail the singular performance of which I had been a witness in the late moonlight before that morning's dawn. As I talked, we half unconsciously moved across the lawn together, finally seating ourselves upon a bench beyond the rose-beds and near the high fence. The interest my companion exhibited in the narration might have surprised me had my nocturnal experience itself been less surprising. She interrupted me now and then with little, half-checked ejaculations of acute wonder, but sat for the most part with her elbow on her knee and her chin in her hand, her face turned eagerly to mine and her lips parted in half-breathless attention. There was nothing "far away" about her eyes now; they were widely and intently alert.

When I finished, she shook her head slowly, as if quite dumfounded, and altered her position, leaning against the back of the bench and gazing straight before her without speaking. It was plain that her neighbor's extraordinary behavior had revealed a phase of his character novel enough to be startling.

"One explanation might be just barely possible," I said. "If it is, it is the most remarkable case of somnambulism on record. Did you ever hear of Mr. Beasley's walking in his—"

She touched me lightly but peremptorily on the arm in warning, and I stopped. On the other side of the board fence a door opened creakily, and there sounded a loud and cheerful voice—that of the gentleman in the dressing-gown.

"HERE we come!" it said; "me and big Bill Hammersley. I want to show Bill I can jump ANYWAYS three times as far as he can! Come on, Bill."

"Is that Mr. Beasley's voice?" I asked, under my breath.

Miss Apperthwaite nodded in affirmation.

"Could he have heard me?"

"No," she whispered. "He's just come out of the house." And then to herself, "Who under heaven is Bill Hammersley? I never heard of HIM!"

"Of course, Bill," said the voice beyond the fence, "if you're afraid I'll beat you TOO badly, you've still got time to back out. I did understand you to kind of hint that you were considerable of a jumper, but if—What? What'd you say, Bill?" There ensued a moment's complete silence. "Oh, all right," the voice then continued. "You say you're in this to win, do you? Well, so'm I, Bill Hammersley; so'm I. Who'll go first? Me? All right—from the edge of the walk here. Now then! One—two—three! HA!"

A sound came to our ears of some one landing heavily—and at full length, it seemed—on the turf, followed by a slight, rusty groan in the same voice. "Ugh! Don't you laugh, Bill Hammersley! I haven't jumped as much as I OUGHT to, these last twenty years; I reckon I've kind of lost the hang of it. Aha!" There were indications that Mr. Beasley was picking himself up, and brushing his trousers with his hands. "Now, it's your turn, Bill. What say?" Silence again, followed by, "Yes, I'll make Simpledoria get out of the way. Come here, Simpledoria. Now, Bill, put your heels together on the edge of the walk. That's right. All ready? Now then! One for the money—two for the show—three to make ready—and four for to GO!" Another silence. "By jingo, Bill Hammersley, you've beat me! Ha, ha! That WAS a jump! What say?" Silence once more. "You say you can do even better than that? Now, Bill, don't brag. Oh! you say you've often jumped farther? Oh! you say that was up in

Scotland, where you had a spring-board? Oho! All right; let's see how far you can jump when you really try. There! Heels on the walk again. That's right; swing your arms. One—two—three! THERE you go!" Another silence. "ZING! Well, sir, I'll be e-tarnally snitched to flinders if you didn't do it THAT time, Bill Hammersley! I see I never really saw any jumping before in all my born days. It's eleven feet if it's an inch. What? You say you—"

I heard no more, for Miss Apperthwaite, her face flushed and her eyes shining, beckoned me imperiously to follow her, and departed so hurriedly that it might be said she ran.

"I don't know," said I, keeping at her elbow, "whether it's more like Alice or the interlocutor's conversation at a minstrel show."

"Hush!" she warned me, though we were already at a safe distance, and did not speak again until we had reached the front walk. There she paused, and I noted that she was trembling—and, no doubt correctly, judged her emotion to be that of consternation.

"There was no one THERE!" she exclaimed. "He was all by himself! It was just the same as what you saw last night!"

"Evidently."

"Did it sound to you"—there was a little awed tremor in her voice that I found very appealing—"did it sound to you like a person who'd lost his MIND?"

"I don't know," I said. "I don't know at all what to make of it."

"He couldn't have been"—her eyes grew very wide—"intoxicated!"

"No. I'm sure it wasn't that."

"Then *I* don't know what to make of it, either. All that wild talk about 'Bill Hammersley' and 'Simpledoria' and spring-boards in Scotland and—"

"And an eleven-foot jump," I suggested.

"Why, there's no more a 'Bill Hammersley,'" she cried, with a gesture of excited emphasis, "than there is a 'Simpledoria'!"

"So it appears," I agreed.

"He's lived there all alone," she said, solemnly, "in that big house, so long, just sitting there evening after evening all by himself, never going out, never reading anything, not even thinking; but just sitting and sitting and sitting and SITTING—Well," she broke off, suddenly, shook the frown from her forehead, and made me the offer of a dazzling smile, "there's no use bothering one's own head about it."

"I'm glad to have a fellow-witness," I said. "It's so eerie I might have concluded there was something the matter with ME."

"You're going to your work?" she asked, as I turned toward the gate. "I'm very glad I don't have to go to mine."

"Yours?" I inquired, rather blankly.

"I teach algebra and plain geometry at the High School," said this surprising young woman. "Thank Heaven, it's Saturday! I'm reading Les Miserables for the seventh time, and I'm going to have a real ORGY over Gervaise and the barricade this afternoon!"

III

I do not know why it should have astonished me to find that Miss Apperthwaite was a teacher of mathematics except that (to my inexperienced eye) she didn't look it. She looked more like Charlotte Corday!

I had the pleasure of seeing her opposite me at lunch the next day (when Mr. Dowden kept me occupied with Spencerville politics, obviously from fear that I would break out again), but no stroll in the yard with her rewarded me afterward, as I dimly hoped, for she disappeared before I left the table, and I did not see her again for a fortnight. On week-days she did not return to the house for lunch, my only meal at Mrs. Apperthwaite's (I dined at a restaurant near the "Despatch" office), and she was out of town for a little visit, her mother informed us, over the following Saturday and Sunday. She was not altogether out of my thoughts, however—indeed, she almost divided them with the Honorable David Beasley.

A better view which I was afforded of this gentleman did not lessen my interest in him; increased it rather; it also served to make the extraordinary didoes of which he had been the virtuoso and I the audience more than ever profoundly inexplicable. My glimpse of him in the lighted doorway had given me the vaguest impression of his appearance, but one afternoon—a few days after my interview with Miss Apperthwaite—I was starting for the office and met him full-face-on as he was turning in at his gate. I took as careful invoice of him as I could without conspicuously glaring.

There was something remarkably "taking," as we say, about this man—something easy and genial and quizzical and careless. He was the kind of person you LIKE to meet on the street; whose cheerful passing sends you on feeling indefinably a little gayer than you did. He was tall, thin—even gaunt, perhaps—and his face was long, rather pale, and shrewd and gentle; something in its oddity not unremindful of the late Sol Smith Russell. His hat was tilted back a little, the slightest bit to one side, and the sparse, brownish hair above his high forehead was going to be gray before long. He looked about forty.

The truth is, I had expected to see a cousin german to Don Quixote; I had thought to detect signs and gleams of wildness, however slight—something a little "off." One glance of that kindly and humorous eye told me such expectation had been nonsense. Odd he might have been—Gadzooks! he looked it—but "queer"? Never. The fact that Miss Apperthwaite could picture such a man as this "sitting and sitting and sitting" himself into any form of mania or madness whatever spoke loudly of her own imagination, indeed! The key to "Simpledoria" was to be sought under some other mat.

... As I began to know some of my co-laborers on the "Despatch," and to pick up acquaintances, here and there, about town, I sometimes made Mr. Beasley the subject of inquiry. Everybody knew him. "Oh yes, I know Dave BEASLEY!" would come the reply, nearly always with a chuckling sort of laugh. I gathered that he had a name for "easy-going" which amounted to eccentricity. It was said that what the ward-heelers and camp-followers got out of him in campaign times made the political managers cry. He was the first and readiest prey for every fraud and swindler that came to Wainwright, I heard, and yet, in spite of this and of his hatred of "speech-making" ("He's as silent as Grant!" said one informant), he had a large practice, and was one of the most successful lawyers in the state.

One story they told of him (or, as they were more apt to put it, "on" him) was repeated so often that I saw it had become one of the town's traditions. One bitter evening in February, they related, he was approached upon the street by a ragged, whining, and shivering old reprobate, notorious for the various ingenuities by which he had worn out the patience of the charity organizations. He asked Beasley for a dime. Beasley had no money in his pockets, but gave the man his overcoat, went home without any himself, and spent six weeks in bed with a bad case of pneumonia as the direct result. His beneficiary sold the overcoat, and invested the proceeds in a five-day's spree, in the closing scenes of which a couple of brickbats were featured to high, spectacular effect. One he sent through a jeweller's show-window in an attempt to intimidate some wholly imaginary pursuers, the other he projected at a perfectly actual policeman who was endeavoring to soothe him. The victim of Beasley's charity and the officer were then borne to the hospital in company.

It was due in part to recollections of this legend and others of a similar character that people laughed when they said, "Oh yes, I know Dave BEASLEY!"

Altogether, I should say, Beasley was about the most popular man in Wainwright. I could discover nowhere anything, however, to shed the faintest light upon the mystery of Bill Hammersley and Simpledoria. It was not until the Sunday of Miss Apperthwaite's absence that the revelation came.

That afternoon I went to call upon the widow of a second-cousin of mine; she lived in a cottage not far from Mrs. Apperthwaite's, upon the same street. I found her sitting on a pleasant veranda, with boxes of flowering plants along the railing, though Indian summer was now close upon departure. She was rocking meditatively, and held a finger in a morocco volume, apparently of verse, though I suspected she had been better entertained in the observation of the people and vehicles decorously passing along the sunlit thoroughfare within her view.

We exchanged inevitable questions and news of mutual relatives; I had told her how I liked my work and what I thought of Wainwright, and she was congratulating me upon having found so pleasant a place to live as Mrs. Apperthwaite's, when she interrupted herself to smile and nod a cordial greeting to two gentlemen driving by in a phaeton. They waved their hats to her gayly, then leaned back comfortably against the cushions—and if ever two men were obviously and incontestably on the best of terms with each other, THESE two were. They were David Beasley and Mr. Dowden. "I do wish," said my cousin, resuming her rocking—"I do wish dear David Beasley would get a new trap of some kind; that old phaeton of his is a disgrace! I suppose you haven't met him? Of course, living at Mrs. Apperthwaite's, you wouldn't be apt to."

"But what is he doing with Mr. Dowden?" I asked.

She lifted her eyebrows. "Why—taking him for a drive, I suppose."

"No. I mean—how do they happen to be together?"

"Why shouldn't they be? They're old friends—"

"They ARE!" And, in answer to her look of surprise, I explained that I had begun to speak of Beasley at Mrs. Apperthwaite's, and described the abruptness with which Dowden had changed the subject.

"I see," my cousin nodded, comprehendingly. "That's simple enough. George Dowden didn't want you to talk of Beasley THERE. I suppose it may have been a little embarrassing for everybody—especially if Ann Apperthwaite heard you."

"Ann? That's Miss Apperthwaite? Yes; I was speaking directly to her. Why SHOULDN'T she have heard me? She talked of him herself a little later—and at some length, too."

"She DID!" My cousin stopped rocking, and fixed me with her glittering eye. "Well, of all!"

"Is it so surprising?"

The lady gave her boat to the waves again. "Ann Apperthwaite thinks about him still!" she said, with something like vindictiveness. "I've always suspected it. She thought you were new to the place and didn't know anything about it all, or anybody to mention it to. That's it!"

"I'm still new to the place," I urged, "and still don't know anything about it all."

"They used to be engaged," was her succinct and emphatic answer.

I found it but too illuminating. "Oh, oh!" I cried. "I WAS an innocent, wasn't I?"

"I'm glad she DOES think of him," said my cousin. "It serves her right. I only hope HE won't find it out, because he's a poor, faithful creature; he'd jump at the chance to take her back—and she doesn't deserve him."

"How long has it been," I asked, "since they used to be engaged?"

"Oh, a good while—five or six years ago, I think—maybe more; time skips along. Ann Apperthwaite's no chicken, you know." (Such was the lady's expression.) "They got engaged just after she came home from college, and of all the idiotically romantic girls—"

"But she's a teacher," I interrupted, "of mathematics."

"Yes." She nodded wisely. "I always thought that explained it: the romance is a reaction from the algebra. I never knew a person connected with mathematics or astronomy or statistics, or any of those exact things, who didn't have a crazy streak in 'em SOMEwhere. They've got to blow off steam and be foolish to make up for putting in so much of their time at hard sense. But don't you think that I dislike Ann Apperthwaite. She's always been one of my best friends; that's why I feel at liberty to abuse her—and I always will abuse her when I think how she treated poor David Beasley."

"How did she treat him?"

"Threw him over out of a clear sky one night, that's all. Just sent him home and broke his heart; that is, it would have been broken if he'd had any kind of disposition except the one the Lord blessed him with—just all optimism and cheerfulness and make-the-best-of-it-ness! He's never cared for anybody else, and I guess he never will."

"What did she do it for?"

"NOTHING!" My cousin shot the indignant word from her lips. "Nothing in the wide WORLD!"

"But there must have been—"

"Listen to me," she interrupted, "and tell me if you ever heard anything queerer in your life. They'd been engaged—Heaven knows how long—over two years; probably nearer three—and always she kept putting it off; wouldn't begin to get ready, wouldn't set a day for the wedding. Then Mr. Apperthwaite died, and left her and her mother stranded high and dry with nothing to live on. David had everything in the world to give her—and STILL she wouldn't! And then, one day, she came up here and told me she'd broken it off. Said she couldn't stand it to be engaged to David Beasley another minute!"

"But why?"

"Because"—my cousin's tone was shrill with her despair of expressing the satire she would have put into it—"because, she said he was a man of no imagination!"

"She still says so," I remarked, thoughtfully.

"Then it's time she got a little imagination herself!" snapped my companion. "David Beasley's the quietest man God has made, but everybody knows what he IS! There are some rare people in this world that aren't all TALK; there are some still rarer ones that scarcely ever talk at all—and David Beasley's one of them. I don't know whether it's because he can't talk, or if he can and hates to; I only know he doesn't. And I'm glad of it, and thank the Lord he's put a few like that into this talky world! David Beasley's smile is better than acres of other people's talk. My Providence! Wouldn't anybody, just to look at him, know that he does better than talk? He THINKS! The trouble with Ann Apperthwaite was that she was too young to see it. She was so full of novels and poetry and dreaminess and highfalutin nonsense she couldn't see ANYTHING as it really was. She'd study her mirror, and see such a heroine of romance there that she just couldn't bear to have a fiance who hadn't any chance of turning out to be the crown-prince of Kenosha in disguise! At the very least, to suit HER he'd have had to wear a 'well-trimmed Vandyke' and coo sonnets in the gloaming, or read On a Balcony to her by a red lamp.

“Poor David! Outside of his law-books, I don't believe he's ever read anything but Robinson Crusoe and the Bible and Mark Twain. Oh, you should have heard her talk about it!—'I couldn't bear it another day,' she said, 'I couldn't STAND it! In all the time I've known him I don't believe he's ever asked me a single question—except when he asked if I'd marry him. He never says ANYTHING—never speaks at ALL!' she said. 'You don't know a blessing when you see it,' I told her. 'Blessing!' she said. 'There's nothing IN the man! He has no DEPTHS! He hasn't any more imagination than the chair he sits and sits and sits in! Half the time he answers what I say to him by nodding and saying 'um-hum,' with that same old foolish, contented smile of his. I'd have gone MAD if it had lasted any longer!' I asked her if she thought married life consisted very largely of conversations between husband and wife; and she answered that even married life ought to have some POETRY in it. 'Some romance,' she said, 'some soul! And he just comes and sits,' she said, 'and sits and sits and sits and sits! And I can't bear it any longer, and I've told him so.'"

"Poor Mr. Beasley," I said.

"*I* think, 'Poor Ann Apperthwaite!'" retorted my cousin. "I'd like to know if there's anything NICER than just to sit and sit and sit and sit with as lovely a man as that—a man who understands things, and thinks and listens and smiles—instead of everlastingly talking!"

"As it happens," I remarked, "I've heard Mr. Beasley talk."

"Why, of course he talks," she returned, "when there's any real use in it. And he talks to children; he's THAT kind of man."

"I meant a particular instance," I began; meaning to see if she could give me any clew to Bill Hammersley and Simpledoria, but at that moment the gate clicked under the hand of another caller. My cousin rose to greet him; and presently I took my leave without having been able to get back upon the subject of Beasley.

Thus, once more baffled, I returned to Mrs. Apperthwaite's—and within the hour came into full possession of the very heart of that dark and subtle mystery which overhung the house next door and so perplexed my soul.

IV

Finding that I had still some leisure before me, I got a book from my room and repaired to the bench in the garden. But I did not read; I had but opened the book when my attention was arrested by sounds from the other side of the high fence—low and tremulous croonings of distinctly African derivation:

"Ah met mah sistuh in a-mawnin', She 'uz a-waggin' up de hill SO slow! 'Sistuh, you mus' git a rastle in doo time, B'fo de hevumly do's cloze—iz!'"

It was the voice of an aged negro; and the simultaneous slight creaking of a small hub and axle seemed to indicate that he was pushing or pulling a child's wagon or perambulator up and down the walk from the kitchen door to the stable. Whiles, he proffered soothing music: over and over he repeated the chant, though with variations; encountering in turn his brother, his daughter, each of his parents, his uncle, his cousin, and his second-cousin, one after the other ascending the same slope with the same perilous leisure.

"Lay still, honey." He interrupted his injunctions to the second-cousin. "Des keep on a-nappin' an' a-breavin' de f'esh air. Dass wha's go' mek you good an' well agin."

Then there spoke the strangest voice that ever fell upon my ear; it was not like a child's, neither was it like a very old person's voice; it might have been a grasshopper's, it was so thin and little, and made of such tiny wavers and quavers and creakings.

"I—want—" said this elfin voice, "I—want—Bill—Hammersley!"

The shabby phaeton which had passed my cousin's house was drawing up to the curb near Beasley's gate. Evidently the old negro saw it.

"Hi dar!" he exclaimed. "Look at dat! Hain' Bill a comin' yonnah des edzacly on de dot an' to de vey spot an' instink when you 'quiah fo' 'im, honey? Dar come Mist' Dave, right on de minute, an' you kin bet yo' las hunnud dollahs he got dat Bill Hammersley wif 'im! Come along, honey-chile! Ah's go' to pull you 'roun in de side yod fo' to meet 'em."

The small wagon creaked away, the chant resuming as it went.

Mr. Dowden jumped out of the phaeton with a wave of his hand to the driver, Beasley himself, who clucked to the horse and drove through his open carriage-gates and down the drive on the other side of the house, where he was lost to my view.

Dowden, entering our own gate, nodded in a friendly fashion to me, and I advanced to meet him.

"Some day I want to take you over next door," he said, cordially, as I came up. "You ought to know Beasley, especially as I hear you're doing some political reporting. Dave Beasley's going to be the next governor of this state, you know." He laughed, offered me a cigar, and we sat down together on the front steps.

"From all I hear," I rejoined, "YOU ought to know who'll get it." (It was said in town that Dowden would "come pretty near having the nomination in his pocket.")

"I expect you thought I shifted the subject pretty briskly the other day?" He glanced at me quizzically from under the brim of his black felt hat. "I meant to tell you about that, but the opportunity didn't occur. You see—"

"I understand," I interrupted. "I've heard the story. You thought it might be embarrassing to Miss Apperthwaite."

"I expect I was pretty clumsy about it," said Dowden, cheerfully. "Well, well—" he flicked his cigar with a smothered ejaculation that was half a sigh and half a laugh; "it's a mighty strange case. Here they keep on living next door to each other, year after year, each going on alone when they might just as well—" He left the sentence unfinished, save for a vocal click of compassion. "They bow when they happen to meet, but they haven't exchanged a word since the night she sent him away, long ago." He shook his head, then his countenance cleared and he chuckled. "Well, sir, Dave's got something at home to keep him busy enough, these days, I expect!"

"Do you mind telling me?" I inquired. "Is its name 'Simpledoria'?"

Mr. Dowden threw back his head and laughed loudly. "Lord, no! What on earth made you think that?"

I told him. It was my second success with this narrative; however, there was a difference: my former auditor listened with flushed and breathless excitement, whereas the present one laughed consumedly throughout. Especially he laughed with a great laughter at the picture of Beasley's coming down at four in the morning to open the door for nothing on sea or land or in the waters under the earth. I gave account, also, of the miraculous jumping contest (though I did not mention Miss Apperthwaite's having been with me), and of the elfin voice I had just now overheard demanding "Bill Hammersley."

"So I expect you must have decided," he chuckled, when I concluded, "that David Beasley has gone just plain, plum insane."

"Not a bit of it. Nobody could look at him and not know better than that."

"You're right THERE!" said Dowden, heartily. "And now I'll tell you all there is TO it. You see, Dave grew up with a cousin of his named Hamilton Swift; they were boys together; went to the same school, and then to college. I don't believe there was ever a high word spoken between them. Nobody in this life ever got a quarrel out of Dave Beasley, and Hamilton Swift was a mighty good sort of a fellow, too. He went East to live, after they got out of college, yet they always managed to get together once a year, generally about Christmas-time; you couldn't pass them on the street without hearing their laughter ringing out louder than the sleigh-bells, maybe over some old joke between them, or some fool thing they did, perhaps, when they were boys. But finally Hamilton Swift's business took him over to the other side of the water to live; and he married an English girl, an orphan without any kin. That was about seven years ago. Well, sir, this last summer he and his wife were taking a trip down in Switzerland, and they were both drowned—tipped over out of a rowboat in Lake Lucerne—and word came that Hamilton Swift's will appointed Dave guardian of the one child they had, a little boy—Hamilton Swift, Junior's his name. He was sent across the ocean in charge of a doctor, and Dave went on to New York to meet him. He brought him home here the very day before you passed the house and saw poor Dave getting up at four in the morning to let that ghost in. And a mighty funny ghost Simpledoria is!"

"I begin to understand," I said, "and to feel pretty silly, too."

"Not at all," he rejoined, heartily. "That little chap's freaks would mystify anybody, especially with Dave humoring 'em the ridiculous way he does. Hamilton Swift, Junior, is the curiousest child I ever saw—and the good Lord knows He made all children powerful mysterious! This poor little cuss has a complication of infirmities that have kept him on his back most of his life, never knowing other children, never playing, or anything; and he's got ideas and ways that I never saw the beat of! He was born sick, as I understand it—his bones and nerves and insides are all wrong, somehow—but it's supposed he gets a little better from year to year. He wears a pretty elaborate set of braces, and he's subject to attacks, too—I don't know the name for 'em—and loses what little voice he has sometimes, all but a whisper. He had one, I know, the day after Beasley brought him home, and that was probably the reason you thought Dave was carrying on all to himself about that jumping-match out in the back-yard. The boy must have been lying there in the little wagon they have for him, while Dave cut up shines with 'Bill Hammersley.' Of course, most children have make-believe friends and companions, especially if they haven't any brothers or sisters, but this lonely little feller's got HIS people worked out in his mind and materialized beyond any I ever heard of. Dave got well acquainted with 'em on the train on the way home, and they certainly are giving him a lively time. Ho, ho! Getting him up at four in the morning—"

Mr. Dowden's mirth overcame him for a moment; when he had mastered it, he continued: "Simpledoria—now where do you suppose he got that name?—well, anyway, Simpledoria is supposed to be Hamilton Swift, Junior's St. Bernard dog. Beasley had to BATHE him the other day, he told me! And Bill Hammersley is supposed to be a boy of Hamilton Swift, Junior's own age, but very big and strong; he has rosy cheeks, and he can do more in athletics than a whole college track-team. That's the reason he outjumped Dave so far, you see."

V

Miss Apperthwaite was at home the following Saturday. I found her in the library with Les Miserables on her knee when I came down from my room a little before lunch-time; and she looked up and gave me a smile that made me feel sorry for any one she had ceased to smile upon.

"I wanted to tell you," I said, with a little awkwardness but plenty of truth, "I've found out that I'm an awful fool."

"But that's something," she returned, encouragingly—"at least the beginning of wisdom."

"I mean about Mr. Beasley—the mystery I was absurd enough to find in 'Simpledoria.' I want to tell you—"

"Oh, *I* know," she said; and although she laughed with an effect of carelessness, that look which I had thought "far away" returned to her eyes as she spoke. There was a certain inscrutability about Miss Apperthwaite sometimes, it should be added, as if she did not like to be too easily read. "I've heard all about it. Mr. Beasley's been appointed trustee or something for poor Hamilton Swift's son, a pitiful little invalid boy who invents all sorts of characters. The old darky from over there told our cook about Bill Hammersley and Simpledoria. So, you see, I understand."

"I'm glad you do," I said.

A little hardness—one might even have thought it bitterness—became apparent in her expression. "And I'm glad there's SOMEbody in that house, at last, with a little imagination!"

"From everything I have heard," I returned, summoning sufficient boldness, "it would be difficult to say which has more—Mr. Beasley or the child."

Her glance fell from mine at this, but not quickly enough to conceal a sudden, half-startled look of trouble (I can think of no other way to express it) that leaped into it; and she rose, for the lunch-bell was ringing.

"I'm just finishing the death of Jean Valjean, you know, in Les Miserables," she said, as we moved to the door. "I'm always afraid I'll cry over that. I try not to, because it makes my eyes red."

And, in truth, there was a vague rumor of tears about her eyes—not as if she had shed them, but more as if she were going to—though I had not noticed it when I came in.

... That afternoon, when I reached the "Despatch" office, I was commissioned to obtain certain political information from the Honorable David Beasley, an assignment I accepted with eagerness, notwithstanding the commiseration it brought me from one or two of my fellows in the reporter's room. "You won't get anything out of HIM!" they said. And they were true prophets.

I found him looking over some documents in his office; a reflective, unlighted cigar in the corner of his mouth; his chair tilted back and his feet on a window-sill. He nodded, upon my statement of the affair that brought me, and, without shifting his position, gave me a look of slow but wholly friendly scrutiny over his shoulder, and bade me sit down. I began at once to put the questions I was told to ask him—interrogations (he seemed to believe) satisfactorily answered by slowly and ruminatively stroking the left side of his chin with two long fingers of his right hand, the while he smiled in genial contemplation of a tarred roof beyond the window. Now and then he would give me a mild and drawling word or two, not brilliantly illuminative, it may be remarked. "Well—about that—" he began once, and came immediately to a full stop.

"Yes?" I said, hopefully, my pencil poised.

"About that—I guess—"

"Yes, Mr. Beasley?" I encouraged him, for he seemed to have dried up permanently.

"Well, sir—I guess—Hadn't you better see some one else about THAT?"

This with the air of a man who would be but too fluent and copious upon any subject in the world except the one particular point.

I never met anybody else who looked so pleasantly communicative and managed to say so little. In fact, he didn't say anything at all; and I guessed that this faculty was not without its value in his political career, disastrous as it had proved to his private happiness. His habit of silence, moreover, was not cultivated: you could see that "the secret of it" was just that he was BORN quiet.

My note-book remained noteless, and finally, at some odd evasion of his, accomplished by a monosyllable, I laughed outright—and he did, too! He joined cachinnations with me heartily, and with a twinkling quizzicalness that somehow gave me the idea that he might be thinking (rather apologetically) to himself: "Yes, sir, that old Beasley man is certainly a mighty funny critter!"

When I went away, a few moments later, and left him still intermittently chuckling, the impression remained with me that he had had some such deprecatory and surreptitious thought.

Two or three days after that, as I started down-town from Mrs. Apperthwaite's, Beasley came out of his gate, bound in the same direction. He gave me a look of gay recognition and offered his hand, saying, "WELL! Up in THIS neighborhood!" as if that were a matter of considerable astonishment.

I mentioned that I was a neighbor, and we walked on together. I don't think he spoke again, except for a "Well, sir!" or two of genial surprise at something I said, and, now and then, "You don't tell me!" which he had a most eloquent way of exclaiming; but he listened visibly to my own talk, and laughed at everything that I meant for funny.

I never knew anybody who gave one a greater responsiveness; he seemed to be WITH you every instant; and HOW he made you feel it was the true mystery of Beasley, this silent man who never talked, except (as my cousin said) to children.

It happened that I thus met him, as we were both starting down-town, and walked on with him, several days in succession; in a word, it became a habit. Then, one afternoon, as I turned to leave him at the "Despatch" office, he asked me if I wouldn't drop in at his house the next day for a cigar before we started. I did; and he asked me if I wouldn't come again the day after that. So this became a habit, too.

A fortnight elapsed before I met Hamilton Swift, Junior; for he, poor little father of dream-children, could be no spectator of track events upon the lawn, but lay in his bed up-stairs. However, he grew better at last, and my presentation took place.

We had just finished our cigars in Beasley's airy, old-fashioned "sitting-room," and were rising to go, when there came the faint creaking of small wheels from the hall. Beasley turned to me with the apologetic and monosyllabic chuckle that was distinctly his alone.

"I've got a little chap here—" he said; then went to the door. "Bob!"

The old darky appeared in the doorway pushing a little wagon like a reclining-chair on wheels, and in it sat Hamilton Swift, Junior.

My first impression of him was that he was all eyes: I couldn't look at anything else for a time, and was hardly conscious of the rest of that weazened, peaked little face and the under-sized wisp of a body with its pathetic adjuncts of metal and leather. I think they were the brightest eyes I ever saw—as keen and intelligent as a wicked old woman's, withal as trustful and cheery as the eyes of a setter pup.

"HOO-ray!"

Thus the Honorable Mr. Beasley, waving a handkerchief thrice around his head and thrice cheering.

And the child, in that cricket's voice of his, replied:

"Br-r-ra-vo!"

This was the form of salutation familiarly in use between them. Beasley followed it by inquiring, "Who's with us to-day?"

"I'm MISTER Swift," chirped the little fellow. "MIS-TER Swift, if you please, Cousin David Beasley."

Beasley executed a formal bow. "There is a gentleman here who'd like to meet you." And he presented me with some grave phrases commendatory of my general character, addressing the child as "Mister Swift"; whereupon Mister Swift gave me a ghostly little hand and professed himself glad to meet me.

"And besides me," he added, to Beasley, "there's Bill Hammersley and Mr. Corley Linbridge."

A faint perplexity manifested itself upon Beasley's face at this, a shadow which cleared at once when I asked if I might not be permitted to meet these personages, remarking that I had heard from Dowden of Bill Hammersley, though until now a stranger to the fame of Mr. Corley Linbridge.

Beasley performed the ceremony with intentional elegance, while the boy's great eyes swept glowingly from his cousin's face to mine and back again. I bowed and shook hands with the air, once to my left and once to my right. "And Simpledoria!" cried Mister Swift. "You'll enjoy Simpledoria."

"Above all things," I said. "Can he shake hands? Some dogs can."

"Watch him!"

Mister Swift lifted a commanding finger. “Simpledoria, shake hands!”

I knelt beside the wagon and shook an imaginary big paw. At this Mister Swift again shook hands with me and allowed me to perceive, in his luminous regard, a solemn commendation and approval.

In this wise was my initiation into the beautiful old house and the cordiality of its inmates completed; and I became a familiar of David Beasley and his ward, with the privilege to go and come as I pleased; there was always gay and friendly welcome. I always came for the cigar after lunch, sometimes for lunch itself; sometimes I dined there instead of down-town; and now and then when it happened that an errand or assignment took me that way in the afternoon, I would run in and “visit” awhile with Hamilton Swift, Junior, and his circle of friends.

There were days, of course, when his attacks were upon him, and only Beasley and the doctor and old Bob saw him; I do not know what the boy's mental condition was at such times; but when he was better, and could be wheeled about the house and again receive callers, he displayed an almost dismaying activity of mind—it was active enough, certainly, to keep far ahead of my own. And he was masterful: still, Beasley and Dowden and I were never directly chidden for insubordination, though made to wince painfully by the look of troubled surprise that met us when we were not quick enough to catch his meaning.

The order of the day with him always began with the “HOO-ray” and “BR-R-RA-vo” of greeting; after which we were to inquire, “Who's with us to-day?” Whereupon he would make known the character in which he elected to be received for the occasion. If he announced himself as "Mister Swift," everything was to be very grown-up and decorous indeed. Formalities and distances were observed; and Mr. Corley Linbridge (an elderly personage of great dignity and distinction as a mountain-climber) was much oftener included in the conversation than Bill Hammersley. If, however, he declared himself to be "Hamilton Swift, Junior," which was his happiest mood, Bill Hammersley and Simpledoria were in the ascendant, and there were games and contests. (Dowden, Beasley, and I all slid down the banisters on one of the Hamilton Swift, Junior, days, at which really picturesque spectacle the boy almost cried with laughter—and old Bob and his wife, who came running from the kitchen, DID cry.) He had a third appellation for himself—"Just little Hamilton"; but this was only when the creaky voice could hardly chirp at all and the weazened face was drawn to one side with suffering. When he told us he was "Just little Hamilton" we were very quiet.

Once, for ten days, his Invisibles all went away on a visit: Hamilton Swift, Junior, had become interested in bears. While this lasted, all of Beasley's trousers were, as Dowden said, "a sight." For that matter, Dowden himself was quite hoarse in court from growling so much. The bears were dismissed abruptly: Bill Hammersley and Mr. Corley Linbridge and Simpledoria came trooping back, and with them they brought that wonderful family, the Hunchbergs.

Beasley had just opened the front door, returning at noon from his office, when Hamilton Swift, Junior's voice came piping from the library, where he was reclining in his wagon by the window.

"Cousin David Beasley! Cousin David, come a-running!" he cried. "Come a-running! The Hunchbergs are here!"

Of course Cousin David Beasley came a-running, and was immediately introduced to the whole Hunchberg family, a ceremony which old Bob, who was with the boy, had previously undergone with courtly grace.

"They like Bob," explained Hamilton. "Don't you, Mr. Hunchberg? Yes, he says they do extremely!" (He used such words as "extremely" often; indeed, as Dowden said, he talked "like a child in a book," which was due, I dare say, to his English mother.) "And I'm sure," the boy went on, "that all the family will admire Cousin David. Yes, Mr. Hunchberg says, he thinks they will."

And then (as Bob told me) he went almost out of his head with joy when Beasley offered Mr. Hunchberg a cigar and struck a match for him to light it.

"But WHAR," exclaimed the old darky, "whar in de name o' de good Gawd do de chile git dem NAMES? Hit lak to SKEER me!"

That was a subject often debated between Dowden and me: there was nothing in Wainwright that could have suggested them, and it did not seem probable he could have remembered them from over the water. In my opinion they were the inventions of that busy and lonely little brain.

I met the Hunchberg family, myself, the day after their arrival, and Beasley, by that time, had become so well acquainted with them that he could remember all their names, and helped in the introductions. There was Mr. Hunchberg—evidently the child's favorite, for he was described as the possessor of every engaging virtue—and there was that lively matron, Mrs. Hunchberg; there were the Hunchberg young gentlemen, Tom, Noble, and Grandee; and the young ladies, Miss Queen, Miss Marble, and Miss Molanna—all exceedingly gay and pretty. There was also Colonel Hunchberg, an uncle; finally there was Aunt Cooley Hunchberg, a somewhat decrepit but very amiable old lady. Mr. Corley Linbridge happened to be calling at the same time; and, as it appeared to be Beasley's duty to keep the conversation going and constantly to include all of the party in its general flow, it struck me that he had truly (as Dowden said) "enough to keep him busy."

The Hunchbergs had lately moved to Wainwright from Constantinople, I learned; they had decided not to live in town, however, having purchased a fine farm out in the country, and, on account of the distance, were able to call at Beasley's only about eight times a day, and seldom more than twice in the evening. Whenever a mystic telephone announced that they were on the way, the child would have himself wheeled to a window; and when they came in sight he would cry out in wild delight, while Beasley hastened to open the front door and admit them.

They were so real to the child, and Beasley treated them with such consistent seriousness, that between the two of them I sometimes began to feel that there actually were such people, and to have moments of half-surprise that I couldn't see them; particularly as each of the Hunchberg's developed a character entirely his own to the last peculiarity, such as the aged Aunt Cooley Hunchberg's deafness, on which account Beasley never once forgot to raise his voice when he addressed her. Indeed, the details of actuality in all this appeared to bring as great a delight to the man as to the child. Certainly he built them up with infinite care. On one occasion when Mr. Hunchberg and I happened to be calling, Hamilton remarked with surprise that Simpledoria had come into the room without licking his hand as he usually did, and had crept under the table. Mr. Hunchberg volunteered the information (through Beasley) that upon his approach to the house he had seen Simpledoria chasing a cat. It was then debated whether chastisement was in order, but finally decided that Simpledoria's surreptitious manner of entrance and his hiding under the table were sufficient indication that he well understood his baseness, and would never let it happen again. And so, Beasley having coaxed him out from under the table, the offender "sat up," begged, and was forgiven. I could almost feel the splendid shaggy head under my hand when, in turn, I patted Simpledoria to show that the reconciliation was unanimous.

VI

Autumn trailed the last leaves behind her flying brown robes one night; we woke to a skurry of snow next morning; and it was winter. Down-town, along the sidewalks, the merchants set lines of poles, covered them with evergreen, and ran streamers of green overhead to encourage the festal shopping. Salvation Army Santa Clauses stamped their feet and rang bells on the corners, and pink-faced children fixed their noses immovably to display-windows. For them, the season of seasons, the time of times, was at hand.

To a certain new reporter on the "Despatch" the stir and gayety of the streets meant little more than that the days had come when it was night in the afternoon, and that he was given fewer political assignments. This was annoying, because Beasley's candidacy for the governorship had given me a personal interest in the political situation. The nominating convention of his party would meet in the spring; the nomination was certain to carry the election also, and thus far Beasley showed more strength than any other man in the field. "Things are looking his way," said Dowden. "He's always worked hard for the party; not on the stump, of course," he laughed; "but the boys understand there are more important things than speech-making. His record in Congress gave him the confidence of everybody in the state, and, besides that, people always trust a quiet man. I tell you if nothing happens he'll get it."

"I'm FER Beasley," another politician explained, in an interview, "because he's Dave Beasley! Yes, sir, I'm FER him. You know the boys say if a man is only FOR you, in this state, there isn't much in it and he may go back on it; but if he's FER you, he means it. Well, I'm FER Beasley!"

There were other candidates, of course; none of them formidable; but I was surprised to learn of the existence of a small but energetic faction opposing our friend in Wainwright, his own town. ("What are you surprised about?" inquired Dowden. "Don't you know what our folks are like, YET? If St. Paul lived in Wainwright, do you suppose he could run for constable without some of his near neighbors getting out to try and down him?")

The head and front (and backbone, too) of the opposition to Beasley was a close-fisted, hard-knuckled, risen-from-the-soil sort of man, one named Simeon Peck. He possessed no inconsiderable influence, I heard; was a hard worker, and vigorously seconded by an energetic lieutenant, a young man named Grist. These, and others they had been able to draw to their faction, were bitterly and eagerly opposed to Beasley's nomination, and worked without ceasing to prevent it.

I quote the invaluable Mr. Dowden again: "Grist's against us because he had a quarrel with a clerk in Beasley's office, and wanted Beasley to discharge him, and Beasley wouldn't; Sim Peck's against us out of just plain wrong-headedness, and because he never was for ANYTHING nor FER anybody in his life. I had a talk with the old mutton-head the other day; he said our candidate ought to be a farmer, a 'man of the common people,' and when I asked him where he'd find anybody more a 'man of the common people' than Beasley, he said Beasley was 'too much of a society man' to suit him! The idea of Dave as a 'society man' was too much for me, and I laughed in Sim Peck's face, but that didn't stop Sim Peck! 'Jest look at the style he lives in,' he yelped. 'Ain't he fairly LAPPED in luxury? Look at that big house he lives in! Look at the way he goes around in that phaeton of his—and a nigger to drive him half the time!' I had to holler again, and, of course, that made Sim twice as mad as he started out to be; and he went off swearing he'd show ME, before the campaign was over. The only trouble he and Grist and that crowd could give us would be by finding out something against Dave, and they can't do that because there isn't anything to find out."

I shared his confidence on this latter score, but was somewhat less sanguine on some others. There were only two newspapers of any political influence in Wainwright, the "Despatch" and the "Journal," both operated in the interest of Beasley's party, and neither had "come out" for him. The gossip I heard about our office led me to think that each was waiting to see what headway Sim Peck and his faction would make; the "Journal" especially, I knew, had some inclination to coquette with Peck, Grist, and Company. Altogether, their faction was not entirely to be despised.

Thus, my thoughts were a great deal more occupied with Beasley's chances than with the holiday spirit that now, with furs and bells and wreathing mists of snow, breathed good cheer over the town. So little, indeed, had this spirit touched me that, one evening when one of my colleagues, standing before the grate-fire in the reporters' room, yawned and said he'd be glad when to-morrow was over, I asked him what was the particular trouble with to-morrow.

"Christmas," he explained, languidly. "Always so tedious. Like Sunday."

"It makes me homesick," said another, a melancholy little man who was forever bragging of his native Duluth.

"Christmas," I repeated—"to-morrow!"

It was Christmas Eve, and I had not known it! I leaned back in my chair in sudden loneliness, what pictures coming before me of long-ago Christmas Eves at home!—old Christmas Eves when there was a Tree....

My name was called; the night City Editor had an assignment for me. "Go up to Sim Peck's, on Madison Street," he said. "He thinks he's got something on David Beasley, but won't say any more over the telephone. See what there is in it."

I picked up my hat and coat, and left the office at a speed which must have given my superior the highest conception of my journalistic zeal. At a telephone station on the next corner I called up Mrs. Apperthwaite's house and asked for Dowden.

"What are you doing?" I demanded, when his voice had responded.

"Playing bridge," he answered.

"Are you going out anywhere?"

"No. What's the trouble?"

"I'll tell you later. I may want to see you before I go back to the office."

"All right. I'll be here all evening."

I hung up the receiver and made off on my errand.

Down-town the streets were crowded with the package-laden people, bending heads and shoulders to the bitter wind, which swept a blinding, sleet-like snow horizontally against them. At corners it struck so tumultuous a blow upon the chest of the pedestrians that for a moment it would halt them, and you could hear them gasping half-smothered "AHS" like bathers in a heavy surf. Yet there was a gayety in this eager gale; the crowds pressed anxiously, yet happily, up and down the street in their generous search for things to give away. It was not the rich who struggled through the storm to-night; these were people who carried their own bundles home. You saw them: toilers and savers, tired mothers and fathers, worn with the grinding thrift of all the year, but now for this one night careless of how hard-saved the money, reckless of everything but the joy of giving it to bring the children joy on the one great to-morrow. So they bent their heads to the freezing wind, their arms laden with daring bundles and their hearts uplifted with the tremulous happiness of giving more than they could afford. Meanwhile, Mr. Simeon Peck, honest man, had chosen this season to work harm if he might to the gentlest of his fellow-men.

I found Mr. Peck waiting for me at his house. There were four other men with him, one of whom I recognized as Grist, a squat young man with slippery-looking black hair and a lambrequin mustache. They were donning their coats and hats in the hall when I arrived.

"From the 'Despatch,' hay?" Mr. Peck gave me greeting, as he wound a knit comforter about his neck. "That's good. We'd most give you up. This here's Mr. Grist, and Mr. Henry P. Cullop, and Mr. Gus Schulmeyer—three men that feel the same way about Dave Beasley that I do. That other young feller," he waved a mittened hand to the fourth man—"he's from the 'Journal.' Likely you're acquainted."

The young man from the 'Journal' was unknown to me; moreover, I was far from overjoyed at his presence.

"I've got you newspaper men here," continued Mr. Peck, "because I'm goin' to show you somep'n' about Dave Beasley that'll open a good many folk's eyes when it's in print."

"Well, what is it?" I asked, rather sharply.

"Jest hold your horses a little bit," he retorted. "Grist and me knows, and so do Mr. Cullop and Mr. Schulmeyer. And I'm goin' to take them and you two reporters to LOOK at it. All ready? Then come on."

He threw open the door, stooped to the gust that took him by the throat, and led the way out into the storm.

“What IS he up to?” I gasped to the “Journal” man as we followed in a straggling line.

“I don't know any more than you do,” he returned. “He thinks he's got something that'll queer Beasley. Peck's an old fool, but it's just possible he's got hold of something. Nearly everybody has ONE thing, at least, that they don't want found out. It may be a good story. Lord, what a night!”

I pushed ahead to the leader's side. “See here, Mr. Peck—” I began, but he cut me off.

“You listen to ME, young man! I'm givin' you some news for your paper, and I'm gittin' at it my own way, but I'll git AT it, don't you worry! I'm goin' to let some folks around here know what kind of a feller Dave Beasley really is; yes, and I'm goin' to show George Dowden he can't laugh at ME!”

“You're going to show Mr. Dowden?” I said. “You mean you're going to take him on this expedition, too?”

“TAKE him!” Mr. Peck emitted an acrid bark of laughter. “I guess HE'S at Beasley's, all right.”

“No, he isn't; he's at home—at Mrs. Apperthwaite's—playing cards.”

“What!”

“I happen to know that he'll be there all evening.”

Mr. Peck smote his palms together. “Grist!” he called, over his shoulder, and his colleague struggled forward. “Listen to this:

even Dowden ain't at Beasley's. Ain't the Lord workin' fer us to-night!"

"Why don't you take Dowden with you," I urged, "if there's anything you want to show him?"

"By George, I WILL!" shouted Peck. "I've got him where the hair's short NOW!"

"That's right," said Grist.

"Gentlemen"—Peck turned to the others—"when we git to Mrs. Apperthwaite's, jest stop outside along the fence a minute. I recken we'll pick up a recruit."

Shivering, we took up our way again in single file, stumbling through drifts that had deepened incredibly within the hour. The wind was straight against us, and so stingingly sharp and so laden with the driving snow that when we reached Mrs. Apperthwaite's gate (which we approached from the north, not passing Beasley's) my eyes were so full of smarting tears I could see only blurred planes of light dancing vaguely in the darkness, instead of brightly lit windows.

"Now," said Peck, panting and turning his back to the wind; "the rest of you gentlemen wait out here. You two newspaper men, you come with me."

He opened the gate and went in, the "Journal" reporter and I following—all three of us wiping our half-blinded eyes. When we reached the shelter of the front porch, I took the key from my pocket and opened the door.

"I live here," I explained to Mr. Peck.

"All right," he said. "Jest step in and tell George Dowden that Sim Peck's out here and wants to see him at the door a minute. Be quick."

I went into the library, and there sat Dowden contemplatively playing bridge with two of the elderly ladies and Miss Apperthwaite. The last-mentioned person quite took my breath away.

In honor of the Christmas Eve (I supposed) she wore an evening dress of black lace, and the only word for what she looked has suffered such misuse that one hesitates over it: yet that is what she was—regal—and no less! There was a sort of splendor about her. It detracted nothing from this that her expression was a little sad: something not uncommon with her lately; a certain melancholy, faint but detectable, like breath on a mirror. I had attributed it to Jean Valjean, though perhaps to-night it might have been due merely to bridge.

"What is it?" asked Dowden, when, after an apology for disturbing the game, I had drawn him out in the hall.

I motioned toward the front door. "Simeon Peck. He thinks he's got something on Mr. Beasley. He's waiting to see you."

Dowden uttered a sharp, half-coherent exclamation and stepped quickly to the door. "Peck!" he said, as he jerked it open.

"Oh, I'm here!" declared that gentleman, stepping into view. "I've come around to let you know that you couldn't laugh like a horse at ME no more, George Dowden! So YOU weren't invited, either."

"Invited?" said Dowden, "Where?"

"Over to the BALL your friend is givin'."

"What friend?"

"Dave Beasley. So you ain't quite good enough to dance with his high-society friends!"

"What are you talking about?" Dowden demanded, impatiently.

"I reckon you won't be quite so strong fer Beasley," responded Peck, with a vindictive little giggle, "when you find he can use you in his BUSINESS, but when it comes to ENTERTAININ'—oh no, you ain't quite the boy!"

"I'd appreciate your explaining," said Dowden. "It's kind of cold standing here."

Peck laughed shrilly. "Then I reckon you better git your hat and coat and come along. Can't do US no harm, and might be an eye-opener fer YOU. Grist and Gus Schulmeyer and Hank Cullop's waitin' out yonder at the gate. We be'n havin' kind of a consultation at my house over somep'n' Grist seen at Beasley's a little earlier in the evening."

"What did Grist see?"

"HACKS! Hacks drivin' up to Beasley's house—a whole lot of 'em. Grist was down the street a piece, and it was pretty dark, but he could see the lamps and hear the doors slam as the people got out. Besides, the whole place is lit up from cellar to attic. Grist come on to my house and told me about it, and I begun usin' the telephone; called up all the men that COUNT in the party—found most of 'em at home, too. I ast 'em if they was invited to this ball to-night; and not a one of 'em was. THEY'RE only in politics; they ain't high SOCIETY enough to be ast to Mr. Beasley's dancin'-parties! But I WOULD 'a' thought he'd let YOU in—ANYWAYS fer the second table!" Mr. Peck shrilled out his acrid and exultant laugh again. "I got these fellers from the newspapers, and all I want is to git this here ball in print to-morrow, and see what the boys that do the work at the primaries have to say about it—and what their WIVES'll say about the man that's too high-toned to have 'em in his house. I'll bet Beasley thought he was goin' to keep these doin's quiet; afraid the farmers might not believe he's jest the plain man he sets up to be—afraid that folks like you that ain't invited might turn against him. I'LL fool him! We're goin' to see what there is to see, and I'm goin' to have these boys from the newspapers write a full account of it. If you want to come along, I expect it'll do you a power o' good."

"I'll go," said Dowden, quickly. He got his coat and hat from a table in the hall, and we rejoined the huddled and shivering group at the gate.

"Got my recruit, gents!" shrilled Peck, slapping Dowden boisterously on the shoulders. "I reckon he'll git a change of heart to-night!"

And now, sheltering my eyes from the stinging wind, I saw what I had been too blind to see as we approached Mrs. Apperthwaite's. Beasley's house WAS illuminated; every window, up stairs and down, was aglow with rosy light. That was luminously evident, although the shades were lowered.

"Look at that!" Peck turned to Dowden, giggling triumphantly. "Wha'd I tell you! How do you feel about it NOW?"

"But where are the hacks?" asked Dowden, gravely.

"Folks all come," answered Mr. Peck, with complete assurance. "Won't be no more hacks till they begin to go home."

We plunged ahead as far as the corner of Beasley's fence, where Peck stopped us again, and we drew together, slapping our hands and stamping our feet. Peck was delighted—a thoroughly happy man; his sour giggle of exultation had become continuous, and the same jovial break was audible in Grist's voice as he said to the "Journal" reporter and me:

"Go ahead, boys. Git your story. We'll wait here fer you."

The "Journal" reporter started toward the gate; he had gone, perhaps, twenty feet when Simeon Peck whistled in sharp warning. The reporter stopped short in his tracks.

Beasley's front door was thrown open, and there stood Beasley himself in evening dress, bowing and smiling, but not at us, for he did not see us. The bright hall behind him was beautiful with evergreen streamers and wreaths, and great flowering plants in jars. A strain of dance-music wandered out to us as the door opened, but there was nobody except David Beasley in sight, which certainly seemed peculiar—for a ball!

"Rest of 'em inside, dancin'," explained Mr. Peck, crouching behind the picket-fence. "I'll bet the house is more'n half full o' low-necked wimmin!"

"Sh!" said Grist. "Listen."

Beasley had begun to speak, and his voice, loud and clear, sounded over the wind. "Come right in, Colonel!" he said. "I'd have sent a carriage for you if you hadn't telephoned me this afternoon that your rheumatism was so bad you didn't expect to be able to come. I'm glad you're well again. Yes, they're all here, and the ladies are getting up a quadrille in the sitting-room."

(It was at this moment that I received upon the calf of the right leg a kick, the ecstatic violence of which led me to attribute it to Mr. Dowden.)

"Gentlemen's dressing-room up-stairs to the right, Colonel," called Beasley, as he closed the door.

There was a pause of awed silence among us.

(I improved it by returning the kick to Mr. Dowden. He made no acknowledgment of its reception other than to sink his chin a little deeper into the collar of his ulster.)

"By the Almighty!" said Simeon Peck, hoarsely. "Who—WHAT was Dave Beasley talkin' to? There wasn't nobody THERE!"

"Git out," Grist bade him; but his tone was perturbed. "He seen that reporter. He was givin' us the laugh."

"He's crazy!" exclaimed Peck, vehemently.

Immediately all four members of his party began to talk at the same time: Mr. Schulmeyer agreeing with Grist, and Mr. Cullop holding with Peck that Beasley had surely become insane; while the "Journal" man, returning, was certain that he had not been seen. Argument became a wrangle; excitement over the remarkable scene we had witnessed, and, perhaps, a certain sharpness partially engendered by the risk of freezing, led to some bitterness. High words were flung upon the wind. Eventually, Simeon Peck got the floor to himself for a moment.

"See here, boys, there's no use gittin' mad amongs' ourselves," he vociferated. "One thing we're all agreed on: nobody here never seen no such a dam peculiar performance as WE jest seen in their whole lives before. THURfore, ball or NO ball, there's somep'n' mighty wrong about this business. Ain't that so?"

They said it was.

"Well, then, there's only one thing to do—let's find out what it is."

"You bet we will."

"I wouldn't send no one in there alone," Peck went on, excitedly, "with a crazy man. Besides, I want to see what's goin' on, myself."—"So do we!" This was unanimous.

"Then let's see if there ain't some way to do it. Perhaps he ain't pulled all the shades down on the other side the house. Lots o' people fergit to do that."

There was but one mind in the party regarding this proposal. The next minute saw us all cautiously sneaking into the side yard, a ragged line of bent and flapping figures, black against the snow.

Simeon Peck's expectations were fulfilled—more than fulfilled. Not only were all the shades of the big, three-faced bay-window of the "sitting-room" lifted, but (evidently on account of the too great generosity of a huge log-fire that blazed in the old-fashioned chimney-place) one of the windows was half-raised as well. Here, in the shadow just beyond the rosy oblongs of light that fell upon the snow, we gathered and looked freely within.

Part of the room was clear to our view, though about half of it was shut off from us by the very king of all Christmas-trees, glittering with dozens and dozens of candles, sumptuous in silver, sparkling in gold, and laden with Heaven alone knows how many and what delectable enticements. Opposite the Tree, his back against the wall, sat old Bob, clad in a dress of state, part of which consisted of a swallow-tail coat (with an overgrown chrysanthemum in the buttonhole), a red necktie, and a pink-and-silver liberty cap of tissue-paper. He was scraping a fiddle "like old times come again," and the tune he played was, "Oh, my Liza, po' gal!" My feet shuffled to it in the snow.

No one except old Bob was to be seen in the room, but we watched him and listened breathlessly. When he finished "Liza," he laid the fiddle across his knee, wiped his face with a new and brilliant blue silk handkerchief, and said:

"Now come de big speech."

The Honorable David Beasley, carrying a small mahogany table, stepped out from beyond the Christmas-tree, advanced to the centre of the room; set the table down; disappeared for a moment and returned with a white water-pitcher and a glass. He placed these upon the table, bowed gracefully several times, then spoke:

"Ladies and gentlemen—" There he paused.

"Well," said Mr. Simeon Peck, slowly, "don't this beat hell!"

"Look out!" The "Journal" reporter twitched his sleeve. "Ladies present."

"Where?" said I.

He leaned nearer me and spoke in a low tone. "Just behind us. She followed us over from your boarding-house. She's been standing around near us all along. I supposed she was Dowden's daughter, probably."

"He hasn't any daughter," I said, and stepped back to the hooded figure I had been too absorbed in our quest to notice.

It was Miss Apperthwaite.

She had thrown a loose cloak over her head and shoulders; but enveloped in it as she was, and crested and epauletted with white, I knew her at once. There was no mistaking her, even in a blizzard.

She caught my hand with a strong, quick pressure, and, bending her head to mine, said, close to my ear:

"I heard everything that man said in our hallway. You left the library door open when you called Mr. Dowden out."

"So," I returned, maliciously, "you—you couldn't HELP following!"

She released my hand—gently, to my surprise.

"Hush," she whispered. "He's saying something."

"Ladies and gentlemen," said Beasley again—and stopped again.

Dowden's voice sounded hysterically in my right ear. (Miss Apperthwaite had whispered in my left.) "The only speech he's ever made in his life—and he's stuck!"

But Beasley wasn't: he was only deliberating.

"Ladies and gentlemen," he began—"Mr. and Mrs. Hunchberg, Colonel Hunchberg and Aunt Cooley Hunchberg, Miss Molanna, Miss Queen, and Miss Marble Hunchberg, Mr. Noble, Mr. Tom, and Mr. Grandee Hunchberg, Mr. Corley Linbridge, and Master Hammersley:—You see before you to-night, my person, merely the representative of your real host. MISTER Swift. Mister Swift has expressed a wish that there should be a speech, and has deputed me to make it. He requests that the subject he has assigned me should be treated in as dignified a manner as is possible—considering the orator. Ladies and gentlemen"—he took a sip of water—"I will now address you upon the following subject: 'Why we Call Christmas-time the Best Time.'

"Christmas-time is the best time because it is the kindest time. Nobody ever felt very happy without feeling very kind, and nobody ever felt very kind without feeling at least a LITTLE happy. So, of course, either way about, the happiest time is the kindest time—that's THIS time. The most beautiful things our eyes can see are the stars; and for that reason, and in remembrance of One star, we set candles on the Tree to be stars in the house. So we make Christmas-time a time of stars indoors; and they shine warmly against the cold outdoors that is like the cold of other seasons not so kind. We set our hundred candles on the Tree and keep them bright throughout the Christmas-time, for while they shine upon us we have light to see this life, not as a battle, but as the march of a mighty Fellowship! Ladies and gentlemen, I thank you!"

He bowed to right and left, as to an audience politely applauding, and, lifting the table and its burden, withdrew;

while old Bob again set his fiddle to his chin and scraped the preliminary measures of a quadrille.

Beasley was back in an instant, shouting as he came: "TAKE your pardners! Balance ALL!"

And then and there, and all by himself, he danced a quadrille, performing at one and the same time for four lively couples. Never in my life have I seen such gyrations and capers as were cut by that long-legged, loose-jointed, miraculously flying figure. He was in the wildest motion without cessation, never the fraction of an instant still; calling the figures at the top of his voice and dancing them simultaneously; his expression anxious but polite (as is the habit of other dancers); his hands extended as if to swing his partner or corner, or "opposite lady"; and his feet lifting high and flapping down in an old-fashioned step. "FIRST four, forward and back!" he shouted. "Forward and SALUTE! BALANCE to corners! SWING pardners! GR-R-RAND Right-and-Left!"

I think the combination of abandon and decorum with which he performed that "Grand Right-and-Left" was the funniest thing I have ever seen. But I didn't laugh at it.

Neither did Miss Apperthwaite.

"NOW do you believe me?" Peck was arguing, fiercely, with Mr. Schulmeyer. "Is he crazy, or ain't he?"

"He is," Grist agreed, hoarsely. "He is a stark, starin', ravin', roarin' lunatic! And the nigger's humorin' him!"

They were all staring, open-mouthed and aghast, into the lighted room.

"Do you see where it puts US?" Simeon Peck's rasping voice rose high.

"I guess I do!" said Grist. "We come out to buy a barn, and got a house and lot fer the same money. It's the greatest night's work you ever done, Sim Peck!"

"I guess it is!"

"Shake on it, Sim."

They shook hands, exalted with triumph.

"This'll do the work," giggled Peck. "It's about two-thousand per cent. better than the story we started to git. Why, Dave Beasley'll be in a padded cell in a month! It'll be all over town to-morrow, and he'll have as much chance fer governor as that nigger in there!" In his ecstasy he smote Dowden deliriously in the ribs. "What do you think of your candidate NOW?"

"Wait," said Dowden. "Who came in the hacks that Grist saw?"

This staggered Mr. Peck. He rubbed his mitten over his woollen cap as if scratching his head. "Why," he said, slowly—"who in Halifax DID come in them hacks?"

"The Hunchbergs," said I.

"Who's the Hunchbergs? Where—"

"Listen," said Dowden.

"FIRST couple, FACE out!" shouted Beasley, facing out with an invisible lady on his akimboed arm, while old Bob sawed madly at A New Coon in Town.

"SECOND couple, FALL in!" Beasley wheeled about and enacted the second couple.

"THIRD couple!" He fell in behind himself again.

"FOURTH couple, IF you please! BALANCE—ALL!—I beg your pardon, Miss Molanna, I'm afraid I stepped on your train.—SASHAY ALL!"

After the "sashay"—the noblest and most dashing bit of gymnastics displayed in the whole quadrille—he bowed profoundly to his invisible partner and came to a pause, wiping his streaming face. Old Bob dexterously swung A New Coon into the stately measures of a triumphal march.

"And now," Beasley announced, in stentorian tones, "if the ladies will be so kind as to take the gentlemen's arms, we will proceed to the dining-room and partake of a slight collation."

Thereupon came a slender piping of joy from that part of the room screened from us by the Tree.

"Oh, Cousin David Beasley, that was the BEAUTIFULLEST quadrille ever danced in the world! And, please, won't YOU take Mrs. Hunchberg out to supper?"

Then into the vision of our paralyzed and dumfounded watchers came the little wagon, pulled by the old colored woman, Bob's wife, in her best, and there, propped upon pillows, lay Hamilton Swift, Junior, his soul shining rapture out of his great eyes, a bright spot of color on each of his thin cheeks. He lifted himself on one elbow, and for an instant something seemed to be wrong with the brace under his chin.

Beasley sprang to him and adjusted it tenderly. Then he bowed elaborately toward the mantel-piece.

"Mrs. Hunchberg," he said, "may I have the honor?" And offered his arm.

"And I must have MISTER Hunchberg," chirped Hamilton. "He must walk with me."

"He tells ME," said Beasley, "he'll be mighty glad to. And there's a plate of bones for Simpledoria."

"You lead the way," cried the child; "you and Mrs. Hunchberg."

"Are we all in line?" Beasley glanced back over his shoulder. "HOO-ray! Now, let us on. Ho! there!"

"BR-R-RA-vo!" applauded Mister Swift.

And Beasley, his head thrown back and his chest out, proudly led the way, stepping nobly and in time to the exhilarating measures. Hamilton Swift, Junior, towed by the beaming old mammy, followed in his wagon, his thin little arm uplifted and his fingers curled as if they held a trusted hand.

When they reached the door, old Bob rose, turned in after them, and, still fiddling, played the procession and himself down the hall.

And so they marched away, and we were left staring into the empty room....

"My soul!" said the "Journal" reporter, gasping. "And he did all THAT—just to please a little sick kid!"

"I can't figure it out," murmured Sim Peck, piteously.

"*I* can," said the "Journal" reporter. "This story WILL be all over town to-morrow." He glanced at me, and I nodded. "It'll be all over town," he continued, "though not in any of the papers—and I don't believe it's going to hurt Dave Beasley's chances any."

Mr. Peck and his companions turned toward the street; they went silently.

The young man from the "Journal" overtook them. "Thank you for sending for me," he said, cordially. "You've given me a treat. I'm FER Beasley!"

Dowden put his hand on my shoulder. He had not observed the third figure still remaining.

"Well, sir," he remarked, shaking the snow from his coat, "they were right about one thing: it certainly was mighty low down of Dave not to invite ME—and you, too—to his Christmas party. Let him go to thunder with his old invitations, I'm going in, anyway! Come on. I'm plum froze."

There was a side door just beyond the bay-window, and Dowden went to it and rang, loud and long. It was Beasley himself who opened it.

"What in the name—" he began, as the ruddy light fell upon Dowden's face and upon me, standing a little way behind. "What ARE you two—snow-banks? What on earth are you fellows doing out here?"

"We've come to your Christmas party, you old horse-thief!" Thus Mr. Dowden.

"HOO-ray!" said Beasley.

Dowden turned to me. "Aren't you coming?"

"What are you waiting for, old fellow?" said Beasley.

I waited a moment longer, and then it happened.

She came out of the shadow and went to the foot of the steps, her cloak falling from her shoulders as she passed me. I picked it up.

She lifted her arms pleadingly, though her head was bent with what seemed to me a beautiful sort of shame. She stood there with the snow driving against her and did not speak. Beasley drew his hand slowly across his eyes—to see if they were really there, I think.

"David," she said, at last. "You've got so many lovely people in your house to-night: isn't there room for—for just one fool? It's Christmas-time!"

Yes, Virginia, There is a Santa Claus

by Francis P. Church (1897)

Letter to the Editor, from Virginia:

Dear Editor,

I am 8 years old. Some of my little friends say that there is no Santa Claus. Papa says "If you see it in the Sun, it is so." Please tell me the truth, is there a Santa Claus?

Letter to Virginia, from the Editor:

Virginia,

Your little friends are wrong. They have been affected by the skepticism of a skeptical age. They do not believe except what they see. They think that nothing can be which is not comprehensible by their little minds.

All minds, Virginia, whether they be men's or children's, are little. In this great universe of ours, man is a mere insect, an ant, in his intellect, as compared with the boundless world about him, as measured by the intelligence capable of grasping the whole of truth and knowledge.

Yes, Virginia, there is a Santa Claus. He exists as certainly as love and generosity and devotion exist, and you know that they abound and give to our life its highest beauty and joy.

Alas! How dreary would be the world if there were no Santa Claus! It would be as dreary as if there were no Virginias. There would be no childlike faith then, no poetry, no romance to make tolerable this existence. We should have no enjoyment, except in sense and sight. The eternal light with which childhood fills the world would be extinguished.

Not believe in Santa Claus? You might as well not believe in fairies! You might get your Papa to hire men to watch all the chimneys on Christmas Eve to catch Santa Claus, but even if they did not see Santa Claus coming down, what would that prove?

Nobody sees Santa Claus, but that is no sign that there is no Santa Claus The most real things in the world are those that neither children nor men can see.

Did you ever see fairies dancing on the lawn? Of course not, but that's no proof that they are not there. Nobody can conceive or imagine all the wonders that are unseen and unseeable in the world.

You tear apart the baby's rattle and see what makes the noise inside, but there is a veil covering the unseen world which not the strongest man, or even the united strength of all the strongest men that ever lived, could tear apart. Only faith, fancy, poetry, love, romance, can push aside that curtain and view and picture the supernatural beauty and glory beyond.

Is it all real? Ah, Virginia, in all this world there is nothing else as real and abiding.

No Santa Claus? Thank God he lives and he lives forever. A thousand years from now, maybe 10 times 10,000 years from now, he will continue to make glad the hearts of children.

The Other Wise Man

by Henry Van Dyke (1895)

The other wise man's name was Artaban. He was one of the Magi and he lived in Persia. He was a man of great wealth, great learning, and great faith. With his learned companions he had searched the scriptures as to the time that the Savior should be born. They knew that a new star would appear and it was agreed between them that Artaban would watch from Persia and the others would observe the sky from Babylon.

On the night he believed the sign was to be given, Artaban went out on this roof to watch the night sky. "If the star appears, they will wait for me ten days, then we will all set out for Jerusalem. I have made ready for the journey by selling all of my possessions and have bought three jewels–a sapphire, a ruby, and a pearl. I intend to present them as my tribute to the king."

As he watched an azure spark was born out of the darkness, rounding itself with splendor into a crimson sphere. Artaban bowed his head. "It is the sign," he said. "The King is coming, and I will go to meet him."

The swiftest of Artaban's horses had been waiting saddled and bridled in her stall, pawing the ground impatiently. She shared the eagerness of her master's purpose.

As Artaban placed himself upon her back, he said, "God bless us both from falling and our souls from death."

They began their journey. Each day his faithful horse measured off the allotted proportion of the distance, and at nightfall on the tenth day, they approached the outskirts of Babylon. In a little island of desert palm trees, Artaban's horse scented difficulty and slackened her pace. Then she stood still, quivering in every muscle.

Artaban dismounted. The dim starlight revealed the from of a man lying in the roadway. His skin bore the mark of a deadly fever. The chill of death was in his lean hand. As Artaban turned to go, a sigh came from the sick man's lips.

Artaban felt sorry that he could not stay to minister to this dying stranger, but this was the hour toward which his entire life and been directed. He could not forfeit the reward of his years of study and faith to do a single deed of human mercy. But then, how could he leave his fellow man alone to die?

"God of truth and mercy," prayed Artaban, "direct me in the path of wisdom which only thou knowest." Then he knew that he could not go on. The Magi were physicians as well as astronomers. He took off his robe and began his work of healing. Several hours later the patient regained consciousness. Artaban gave him all that was left of his bread and wine. He left a potion of healing herbs and instructions for his care.

Though Artaban rode with the greatest haste the rest of the way, it was after dawn that he arrived at the designated meeting place. His friends were nowhere to be seen. Finally his eyes caught a piece of parchment arranged to attract his attention. It said, "We have waited till past midnight, and can delay no longer. We go to find the King. Follow us across the desert." Artaban sat down in despair and covered his face with his hands. "How can I cross the desert with no food and with a spent horse? I must return to Babylon, sell my sapphire and buy camels and provisions for the journey. I may never overtake my friends. Only the merciful God knows whether or not I shall lose my purpose because I tarried to show mercy."

Several days later when Artaban arrived at Bethlehem, the streets were deserted. It was rumored that Herod was sending soldiers, presumably to enforce some new tax, and the men of the city had taken their flocks into the hills beyond his reach.

The door of one dwelling was open, and Artaban could hear a mother singing a lullaby to her child. He entered and introduced himself. The woman told him that it was now the third day since the three wise men had appeared in Bethlehem. They had found Joseph and Mary and the young child, and had laid their gifts at His feet. Then they had gone as mysteriously as they had come. Joseph had taken his wife and babe that same night and had secretly fled. It was whispered that they were going far away into Egypt.

As Artaban listened, the baby reached up its dimpled hand and touched his cheek and smiled. His heart warmed at the touch. Then suddenly, outside there arose a wild confusion of sounds. Women were shrieking. Then a desperate cry was heard, "The soldiers of Herod are killing the children."

Artaban went to the doorway. A band of soldiers came hurrying down the street. The captain approached the door to thrust Artaban aside, but Artaban did not stir. His face was as calm as though he were still watching the stars. Finally his out-stretched hand revealed the giant ruby. He said, "I am waiting to give this jewel to the prudent captain who will go on his way and leave this house alone."

The captain, amazed at the splendor of the gem, took it and said to his men, "March on, there are no children here."

Then Artaban prayed, "Oh, God, forgive me my sin, I have spent for men that which was meant for God. Shall I ever be worthy to see the face of the King?"

But the voice of the woman, weeping for joy in the shadows behind him said softly, "Thou hast saved the life of my little one. May the Lord bless thee and keep thee and give thee peace."

Artaban, still following the King, went on into Egypt seeking everywhere for traces of the little family that had fled before him. For many years we follow Artaban in his search. We see him at the pyramids. We see him in Alexandria taking counsel with a Hebrew rabbi who told him to seek the King not among the rich but among the poor.

He passed through countries where famine lay heavy upon the land, and the poor were crying for bread. He made his dwelling in plague-stricken cities. He visited the oppressed and the afflicted in prisons. He searched the crowded slave-markets. Though he found no one to worship, he found many to serve. As the years passed he fed the hungry, clothed the naked, healed the sick and comforted the captive.

Thirty-three years had now passed away since Artaban began his search. His hair was white as snow. He knew his life's end was near, but he was still desperate with hope that he would find the King. He had come for the last time to Jerusalem.

It was the season of the Passover and the city was thronged with strangers. Artaban inquired where they were going. One answered, "We are going to the execution on Golgotha outside the city walls. Two robbers are going to be crucified, and with them another called Jesus of Nazareth, a man who has done many wonderful works among the people. He claims to be the Son of God and the priests and elders have said that he must die. Pilate sent him to the cross."

How strangely these familiar words fell upon the tired heart of Artaban. They had led him for a lifetime over land and sea. And now they came to him like a message of despair. The King had been denied and cast out. Perhaps he was already dying. Could he be the same one for whom the star had appeared thirty-three long years ago?

Artaban's heart beat loudly within him. He thought, "It may be that I shall yet find the King and be able to ransom him from death by giving my treasure to his enemies."

But as Artaban started toward Calvary, he saw a troop of soldiers coming down the street, dragging a sobbing young woman. As Artaban paused, she broke away from her tormentors and threw herself at his feet, her arms clasped around his knees.

"Have pity on me," she cried. "And save me. My father was also of the Magi, but he is dead. I am to be sold as a slave to pay his debts."

Artaban trembled as he again felt the conflict arising in his soul. It was the same he had experienced in the palm grove of Babylon and in the cottage at Bethlehem. Twice the gift which he had consecrated to the King had been drawn from his hand to the service of humanity. Would he now fail again? One thing was clear, he must rescue this helpless child from evil.

He took the pearl and laid it in the hand of the girl and said, "Daughter, this is the ransom. It is the last of my treasures which I had hoped to keep for the King."

While he spoke, the darkness of the sky thickened and the shuddering tremors of an earthquake ran through the ground. The houses rocked. The soldiers fled in terror. Artaban sank beside a protecting wall. What had he to fear? What had he to hope for? He had given away the last of his tribute to the King. The quest was over and he had failed. What else mattered?

The earthquake quivered beneath him. A heavy tile, shaken from a roof, fell and struck him. He lay breathless and pale. Then there came a still small voice through the twilight. It was like distant music. The rescued girl leaned over him and heard him say, "Not so, my Lord; for when saw I thee hungered and fed thee. Or thirsty and gave thee drink? When saw I thee sick or in prison and came unto thee? Thirty-three years have I looked for thee; but I have never seen thy face, nor ministered unto thee, my King."

The sweet voice came again, "Verily I say unto thee, that inasmuch as thou hast done it unto done of the least of these my brethren, thou hast done it unto me."

A calm radiance of wonder and joy lighted the face of Artaban as one long, last breath exhaled gently from his lips. His journey was ended. His treasure accepted. The Other Wise Man had found the King.

The Burglar's Christmas

by Willa Cather (1896)

Two very shabby looking young men stood at the corner of Prairie avenue and Eightieth street, looking despondently at the carriages that whirled by. It was Christmas Eve, and the streets were full of vehicles; florists' wagons, grocers' carts and car-riages. The streets were in that half-liquid, half-congealed condition peculiar to the streets of Chicago at that season of the year. The swift wheels that spun by sometimes threw the slush of mud and snow over the two young men who were talking on the corner.

"Well," remarked the elder of the two, "I guess we are at our rope's end, sure enough. How do you feel?"

"Pretty shaky. The wind's sharp to-night. If I had had anything to eat I mightn't mind it so much. There is simply no show. I'm sick of the whole business. Looks like there's nothing for it but the lake."

"O, nonsense, I thought you had more grit. Got anything left you can hoc?"

"Nothing but my beard, and I am afraid they wouldn't find it worth a pawn ticket," said the younger man ruefully, rubbing the week's growth of stubble on his face.

"Got any folks anywhere? Now's your time to strike 'em if you have."

"Never mind if I have, they're out of the question."

"Well, you'll be out of it before many hours if you don't make a move of some sort. A man's got to eat. See here, I am going down to Longtin's saloon. I used to play the banjo in there with a couple of coons, and I'll bone him for some of his free lunch stuff. You'd better come along, perhaps they'll fill an order for two."

"How far down is it?"

"Well, it's clear down town, of course, way down on Michigan avenue."

"Thanks, I guess I'll loaf around here. I don't feel equal to the walk, and the cars—well, the cars are crowded." His features drew themselves into what might have been a smile under happier circumstances.

"No, you never did like street cars, you're too aristocratic. See here, Crawford, I don't like leaving you here. You ain't good company for yourself to-night."

"Crawford? O, yes, that's the last one. There have been so many I forget them."

"Have you got a real name, anyway?"

"O, yes, but it's one of the ones I've forgotten. Don't you worry about me. You go along and get your free lunch. I think I had a row in Longtin's place once. I'd better not show myself there again." As he spoke the young man nodded and turned slowly up the avenue.

He was miserable enough to want to be quite alone. Even the crowd that jostled by him annoyed him. He wanted to think about himself. He had avoided this final reckoning with himself for a year now. He had laughed it off and drunk it off. But now, when all those artificial devices which are employed to turn our thoughts into other channels and shield us from ourselves had failed him, it must come. Hunger is a powerful incentive to introspection.

It is a tragic hour, that hour when we are finally driven to reckon with ourselves, when every avenue of mental distraction has been cut off and our own life and all its ineffaceable failures closes about us like the walls of that old torture chamber of the Inquisition. To-night, as this man stood stranded in the streets of the city, his hour came. It was not the first time he had been hungry and desperate and alone. But always before there had been some outlook, some chance ahead, some pleasure yet untasted that seemed worth the effort, some face that he fancied was, or would be, dear. But it was not so to-night. The unyielding conviction was upon him that he had failed in everything, had outlived everything. It had been near him for a long time, that Pale Spectre. He had caught its shadow at the bottom of his glass many a time, at the head of his bed when he was sleepless at night, in the twilight shadows when some great sunset broke upon him. It had made life hateful to him when he awoke in the morning before now. But now it settled slowly over him, like night, the endless Northern nights that bid the sun a long farewell. It rose up before him like granite. From this brilliant city with its glad bustle of Yule-tide he was shut off as completely as though he were a creature of another species. His days seemed numbered and done, sealed over like the little coral cells at the bottom of the sea. Involuntarily he drew that cold air through his lungs slowly, as though he were tasting it for the last time.

Yet he was but four and twenty, this man—he looked even younger—and he had a father some place down East who had been very proud of him once. Well, he had taken his life into his own hands, and this was what he had made of it. That was all there was to be said. He could remember the hopeful things they used to say about him at college in the old days, before he had cut away and begun to live by his wits, and he found courage to smile at them now. They had read him wrongly. He knew now that he never had the essentials of success, only the superficial agility that is often mistaken for it. He was tow without the tinder, and he had burnt himself out at other people's fires. He had helped other people to make it win, but he himself—he had never touched an enterprise that had not failed eventually. Or, if it survived his connection with it, it left him behind.

His last venture had been with some ten-cent specialty company, a little lower than all the others, that had gone to pieces in Buffalo, and he had worked his way to Chicago by boat. When the boat made up its crew for the outward voyage, he was dispensed with as usual. He was used to that. The reason for it? O, there are so many reasons for failure! His was a very common one.

As he stood there in the wet under the street light he drew up his reckoning with the world and decided that it had treated him as well as he deserved. He had overdrawn his account once too often. There had been a day when he thought otherwise; when he had said he was unjustly handled, that his failure was merely the lack of proper adjustment between himself and other men, that some day he would be recognized and it would all come right. But he knew better than that now, and he was still man enough to bear no grudge against any one—man or woman.

To-night was his birthday, too. There seemed something particularly amusing in that. He turned up a limp little coat collar to try to keep a little of the wet chill from his throat, and instinctively began to remember all the birthday parties he used to have. He was so cold and empty that his mind seemed unable to grapple with any serious question. He kept thinking about ginger bread and frosted cakes like a child. He could remember the splendid birthday parties his mother used to give him, when all the other little boys in the block came in their Sunday clothes and creaking shoes, with their ears still red from their mother's towel, and the pink and white birthday cake, and the stuffed olives and all the dishes of which he had been particularly fond, and how he would eat and eat and then go to bed and dream of Santa Claus. And in the morning he would awaken and eat again, until by night the family doctor arrived with his castor oil, and poor William used to dolefully say that it was altogether too much to have your birthday and Christmas all at once. He could remember, too, the royal birthday suppers he had given at college, and the stag dinners, and the toasts, and the music, and the good fellows who had wished him happiness and really meant what they said.

And since then there were other birthday suppers that he could not remember so clearly; the memory of them was heavy and flat, like cigarette smoke that has been shut in a room all night, like champagne that has been a day opened, a song that has been too often sung, an acute sensation that has been overstrained. They seemed tawdry and garish, discordant to him now. He rather wished he could forget them altogether.

Whichever way his mind now turned there was one thought that it could not escape, and that was the idea of food. He caught the scent of a cigar suddenly, and felt a sharp pain in the pit of his abdomen and a sudden moisture in his mouth. His cold hands clenched angrily, and for a moment he felt that bitter hatred of wealth, of ease, of everything that is well-fed and well-housed that is common to starving men. At any rate he had a right to eat! He had demanded great things from the world once: fame and wealth and admiration. Now it was simply bread—and he would have it! He looked about him quickly and felt the blood begin to stir in his veins. In all his straits he had never stolen anything, his tastes were above it. But to-night there would be no to-morrow. He was amused at the way in which the idea excited him. Was it possible there was yet one more experience that would distract him, one thing that had power to excite his jaded interest? Good! he had failed at everything else, now he would see what his chances would be as a common thief. It would be amusing to watch the beautiful consistency of his destiny work itself out even in that role. It would be interesting to add another study to his gallery of futile attempts, and then label them all: "the failure as a journalist," "the failure as a lecturer," "the failure as a business man," "the failure as a thief," and so on, like the titles under the pictures of the Dance of Death. It was time that Childe Roland came to the dark tower.

A girl hastened by him with her arms full of packages. She walked quickly and nervously, keeping well within the shadow, as if she were not accustomed to carrying bundles and did not care to meet any of her friends. As she crossed the muddy street, she made an effort to lift her skirt a little, and as she did so one of the packages slipped unnoticed from beneath her arm. He caught it up and overtook her. "Excuse me, but I think you dropped something."

She started, "O, yes, thank you, I would rather have lost anything than that."

The young man turned angrily upon himself. The package must have contained something of value. Why had he not kept it? Was this the sort of thief he would make? He ground his teeth together. There is nothing more maddening than to have morally consented to crime and then lack the nerve force to carry it out.

A carriage drove up to the house before which he stood. Several richly dressed women alighted and went in. It was a new house, and must have been built since he was in Chicago last. The front door was open and he could see down the hall-way and up the stair case. The servant had left the door and gone with the guests. The first floor was brilliantly lighted, but the windows upstairs were dark. It looked very easy, just to slip upstairs to the darkened chambers where the jewels and trinkets of the fashionable occupants were kept.

Still burning with impatience against himself he entered quickly. Instinctively he removed his mud-stained hat as he passed quickly and quietly up the stair case. It struck him as being a rather superfluous courtesy in a burglar, but he had done it before he had thought. His way was clear enough, he met no one on the stairway or in the upper hall. The gas was lit in the upper hall. He passed the first chamber door through sheer cowardice. The second he entered quickly, thinking of something else lest his courage should fail him, and closed the door behind him. The light from the hall shone into the room through the transom. The apartment was furnished richly enough to justify his expectations. He went at once to the dressing case. A number of rings and small trinkets lay in a silver tray. These he put hastily in his pocket. He opened the upper drawer and found, as he expected, several leather cases. In the first he opened was a lady's watch, in the second a pair of old-fashioned bracelets; he seemed to dimly remember having seen bracelets like them before, somewhere. The third case was heavier, the spring was much worn, and it opened easily. It held a cup of some kind. He held it up to the light and then his strained nerves gave way and he uttered a sharp exclamation. It was the silver mug he used to drink from when he was a little boy.

The door opened, and a woman stood in the doorway facing him. She was a tall woman, with white hair, in evening dress. The light from the hall streamed in upon him, but she was not afraid. She stood looking at him a moment, then she threw out her hand and went quickly toward him.

"Willie, Willie! Is it you!"

He struggled to loose her arms from him, to keep her lips from his cheek. "Mother—you must not! You do not understand! O, my God, this is worst of all!" Hunger, weakness, cold, shame, all came back to him, and shook his self-control completely. Physically he was too weak to stand a shock like this. Why could it not have been an ordinary discovery, arrest, the station house and all the rest of it. Anything but this! A hard dry sob broke from him. Again he strove to disengage himself.

"Who is it says I shall not kiss my son? O, my boy, we have waited so long for this! You have been so long in coming, even I almost gave you up."

Her lips upon his cheek burnt him like fire. He put his hand to his throat, and spoke thickly and incoherently: "You do not understand. I did not know you were here. I came here to rob—it is the first time—I swear it—but I am a common thief. My pockets are full of your jewels now. Can't you hear me? I am a common thief!"

"Hush, my boy, those are ugly words. How could you rob your own house? How could you take what is your own? They are all yours, my son, as wholly yours as my great love—and you can't doubt that, Will, do you?"

That soft voice, the warmth and fragrance of her person stole through his chill, empty veins like a gentle stimulant. He felt as though all his strength were leaving him and even consciousness. He held fast to her and bowed his head on her strong shoulder, and groaned aloud.

"O, mother, life is hard, hard!"

She said nothing, but held him closer. And O, the strength of those white arms that held him! O, the assurance of safety in that warm bosom that rose and fell under his cheek! For a moment they stood so, silently. Then they heard a heavy step upon the stair. She led him to a chair and went out and closed the door. At the top of the staircase she met a tall, broad-shouldered man, with iron gray hair, and a face alert and stern. Her eyes were shining and her cheeks on fire, her whole face was one expression of intense determination.

"James, it is William in there, come home. You must keep him at any cost. If he goes this time, I go with him. O, James, be easy with him, he has suffered so." She broke from a command to an entreaty, and laid her hand on his shoulder. He looked questioningly at her a moment, then went in the room and quietly shut the door.

She stood leaning against the wall, clasping her temples with her hands and listening to the low indistinct sound of the voices within. Her own lips moved silently. She waited a long time, scarcely breathing. At last the door opened, and her husband came out. He stopped to say in a shaken voice,

"You go to him now, he will stay. I will go to my room. I will see him again in the morning."

She put her arm about his neck, "O, James, I thank you, I thank you! This is the night he came so long ago, you remember? I gave him to you then, and now you give him back to me!"

"Don't, Helen," he muttered. "He is my son, I have never forgotten that. I failed with him. I don't like to fail, it cuts my pride. Take him and make a man of him." He passed on down the hall.

She flew into the room where the young man sat with his head bowed upon his knee. She dropped upon her knees beside him. Ah, it was so good to him to feel those arms again!

"He is so glad, Willie, so glad! He may not show it, but he is as happy as I. He never was demonstrative with either of us, you know."

"O, my God, he was good enough," groaned the man. "I told him everything, and he was good enough. I don't see how either of you can look at me, speak to me, touch me." He shivered under her clasp again as when she had first touched him, and tried weakly to throw her off.

But she whispered softly,

"This is my right, my son."

Presently, when he was calmer, she rose. "Now, come with me into the library, and I will have your dinner brought there."

As they went down stairs she remarked apologetically, "I will not call Ellen to-night; she has a number of guests to attend to. She is a big girl now, you know, and came out last winter. Besides, I want you all to myself to-night."

When the dinner came, and it came very soon, he fell upon it savagely. As he ate she told him all that had transpired during the years of his absence, and how his father's business had brought them there. "I was glad when we came. I thought you would drift West. I seemed a good deal nearer to you here."

There was a gentle unobtrusive sadness in her tone that was too soft for a reproach.

"Have you everything you want? It is a comfort to see you eat."

He smiled grimly, "It is certainly a comfort to me. I have not indulged in this frivolous habit for some thirty-five hours."

She caught his hand and pressed it sharply, uttering a quick remonstrance.

"Don't say that! I know, but I can't hear you say it,—it's too terrible! My boy, food has choked me many a time when I have thought of the possibility of that. Now take the old lounging chair by the fire, and if you are too tired to talk, we will just sit and rest together."

He sank into the depths of the big leather chair with the lion's heads on the arms, where he had sat so often in the days when his feet did not touch the floor and he was half afraid of the grim monsters cut in the polished wood. That chair seemed to speak to him of things long forgotten. It was like the touch of an old familiar friend. He felt a sudden yearning tenderness for the happy little boy who had sat there and dreamed of the big world so long ago. Alas, he had been dead many a summer, that little boy!

He sat looking up at the magnificent woman beside him. He had almost forgotten how handsome she was; how lustrous and sad were the eyes that were set under that serene brow, how impetuous and wayward the mouth even now, how superb the white throat and shoulders! Ah, the wit and grace and fineness of this woman! He remembered how proud he had been of her as a boy when she came to see him at school. Then in the deep red coals of the grate he saw the faces of other women who had come since then into his vexed, disordered life. Laughing faces, with eyes artificially bright, eyes without depth or meaning, features without the stamp of high sensibilities. And he had left this face for such as those!

He sighed restlessly and laid his hand on hers. There seemed refuge and protection in the touch of her, as in the old days when he was afraid of the dark. He had been in the dark so long now, his confidence was so thoroughly shaken, and he was bitterly afraid of the night and of himself.

"Ah, mother, you make other things seem so false. You must feel that I owe you an explanation, but I can't make any, even to myself. Ah, but we make poor exchanges in life. I can't make out the riddle of it all. Yet there are things I ought to tell you before I accept your confidence like this."

"I'd rather you wouldn't, Will. Listen: Between you and me there can be no secrets. We are more alike than other people. Dear boy, I know all about it. I am a woman, and circumstances were different with me, but we are of one blood. I have lived all your life before you. You have never had an impulse that I have not known, you have never touched a brink that my feet have not trod. This is your birthday night. Twenty-four years ago I foresaw all this. I was a young woman then and I had hot battles of my own, and I felt your likeness to me. You were not like other babies. From the hour you were born you were restless and discontented, as I had been before you. You used to brace your strong little limbs against mine and try to throw me off as you did to-night. To-night you have come back to me, just as you always did after you ran away to swim in the river that was forbidden you, the river you loved because it was forbidden. You are tired and sleepy, just as you used to be then, only a little older and a little paler and a little more foolish. I never asked you where you had been then, nor will I now. You have come back to me, that's all in all to me. I know your every possibility and limitation, as a composer knows his instrument."

He found no answer that was worthy to give to talk like this. He had not found life easy since he had lived by his wits. He had come to know poverty at close quarters. He had known what it was to be gay with an empty pocket, to wear violets in his button hole when he had not breakfasted, and all the hateful shams of the poverty of idleness. He had been a reporter on a big metropolitan daily, where men grind out their brains on paper until they have not one idea left—and still grind on. He had worked in a real estate office, where ignorant men were swindled. He had sung in a comic opera chorus and played *Harris* in an Uncle Tom's Cabin Company, and edited a Socialist weekly. He had been dogged by debt and hunger and grinding poverty, until to sit here by a warm fire without concern as to how it would be paid for seemed unnatural.

He looked up at her questioningly. "I wonder if you know how much you pardon?"

"O, my poor boy, much or little, what does it matter? Have you wandered so far and paid such a bitter price for knowledge and not yet learned that love has nothing to do with pardon or forgiveness, that it only loves, and loves—and loves? They have not taught you well, the women of your world." She leaned over and kissed him, as no woman had kissed him since he left her.

He drew a long sigh of rich content. The old life, with all its bitterness and useless antagonism and flimsy sophistries, its brief delights that were always tinged with fear and distrust and unfaith, that whole miserable, futile, swindled world of Bohemia seemed immeasurably distant and far away, like a dream that is over and done. And as the chimes rang joyfully outside and sleep pressed heavily upon his eyelids, he wondered dimly if the Author of this sad little riddle of ours were not able to solve it after all, and if the Potter would not finally mete out his all comprehensive justice, such as none but he could have, to his Things of Clay, which are made in his own patterns, weak or strong, for his own ends; and if some day we will not awaken and find that all evil is a dream, a mental distortion that will pass when the dawn shall break.

What the Bells Saw and Said

by Louisa May Alcott (1882)

"Bells ring others to church, but
go not in themselves."

NO one saw the spirits of the bells up there in the old steeple at midnight on Christmas Eve. Six quaint figures, each wrapped in a shadowy cloak and wearing a bell-shaped cap. All were gray-headed, for they were among the oldest bell-spirits of the city, and "the light of other days" shone in their thoughtful eyes. Silently they sat, looking down on the snow-covered roofs glittering in the moonlight, and the quiet streets deserted by all but the watchmen on their chilly rounds, and such poor souls as wandered shelterless in the winter night. Presently one of the spirits said, in a tone, which, low as it was, filled the belfry with reverberating echoes,—

"Well, brothers, are your reports ready of the year that now lies dying?"

All bowed their heads, and one of the oldest answered in a sonorous voice:—

"My report isn't all I could wish. You know I look down on the commercial part of our city and have fine opportunities for seeing what goes on there. It's my business to watch the business men, and upon my word I'm heartily ashamed of them sometimes. During the war they did nobly, giving their time and money, their sons and selves to the good cause, and I was proud of them. But now too many of them have fallen back into the old ways, and their motto seems to be, 'Every one for himself, and the devil take the hindmost.' Cheating, lying and stealing are hard words, and I don't mean to apply them to *all* who swarm about below there like ants on an ant-hill—*they* have other names for these things, but I'm old-fashioned and use plain words. There's a deal too much dishonesty in the world, and business seems to have become a game of hazard in which luck, not labor, wins the prize. When I was young, men were years making moderate fortunes, and were satisfied with them. They built them on sure foundations, knew how to enjoy them while they lived, and to leave a good name behind them when they died.

"Now it's anything for money; health, happiness, honor, life itself, are flung down on that great gaming-table, and they forget everything else in the excitement of success or the desperation of defeat. Nobody seems satisfied either, for those who win have little time or taste to enjoy their prosperity, and those who lose have little courage or patience to support them in adversity. They don't even fail as they used to. In my day when a merchant found himself embarrassed he didn't ruin others in order to save himself, but honestly confessed the truth, gave up everything, and began again. But now-a-days after all manner of dishonorable shifts there comes a grand crash; many suffer, but by some hocus-pocus the merchant saves enough to retire upon and live comfortably here or abroad. It's very evident that honor and honesty don't mean now what they used to mean in the days of old May, Higginson and Lawrence.

"They preach below here, and very well too sometimes, for I often slide down the rope to peep and listen during service. But, bless you! they don't seem to lay either sermon, psalm or prayer to heart, for while the minister is doing his best, the congregation, tired with the breathless hurry of the week, sleep peacefully, calculate their chances for the morrow, or wonder which of their neighbors will lose or win in the great game. Don't tell me! I've seen them do it, and if I dared I'd have startled every soul of them with a rousing peal. Ah, they don't dream whose eye is on them, they never guess what secrets the telegraph wires tell as the messages fly by, and little know what a report I give to the winds of heaven as I ring out above them morning, noon, and night." And the old spirit shook his head till the tassel on his cap jangled like a little bell.

"There are some, however, whom I love and honor," he said, in a benignant tone, "who honestly earn their bread, who deserve all the success that comes to them, and always keep a warm corner in their noble hearts for those less blest than they. These are the men who serve the city in times of peace, save it in times of war, deserve the highest honors in its gift, and leave behind them a record that keeps their memories green. For such an one we lately tolled a knell, my brothers; and as our united voices pealed over the city, in all grateful hearts, sweeter and more solemn than any chime, rung the words that made him so beloved,—

"'Treat our dead boys tenderly, and send them home to me.'"

He ceased, and all the spirits reverently uncovered their gray heads as a strain of music floated up from the sleeping city and died among the stars.

"Like yours, my report is not satisfactory in all respects," began the second spirit, who wore a very pointed cap and a finely-ornamented cloak. But, though his dress was fresh and youthful, his face was old, and he had nodded several times during his brother's speech. "My greatest affliction during the past year has been the terrible extravagance which prevails. My post, as you know, is at the court end of the city, and I see all the fashionable vices and follies. It is a marvel to me how so many of these immortal creatures, with such opportunities for usefulness, self-improvement and genuine happiness can be content to go round and round in one narrow circle of unprofitable and unsatisfactory pursuits. I do my best to warn them; Sunday after Sunday I chime in their ears the beautiful old hymns that sweetly chide or cheer the hearts that truly listen and believe; Sunday after Sunday I look down on them as they pass in, hoping to see that my words have not fallen upon deaf ears; and Sunday after Sunday they listen to words that should teach them much, yet seem to go by them like the wind. They are told to love their neighbor, yet too many hate him because he possesses more of this world's goods or honors than they; they are told that a rich man cannot enter the kingdom of heaven, yet they go on laying up perishable wealth, and though often warned that moth and rust will corrupt, they fail to believe it till the worm that destroys enters and mars their own chapel of ease. Being a spirit, I see below external splendor and find much poverty of heart and soul under the velvet and the ermine which should cover rich and royal natures. Our city saints walk abroad in threadbare suits, and under quiet bonnets shine the eyes that make sunshine in the shady places. Often as I watch the glittering procession passing to and fro below me, I wonder if, with all our progress, there is to-day as much real piety as in the times when our fathers, poorly clad, with weapon in one hand and Bible in the other, came weary distances to worship in the wilderness with fervent faith unquenched by danger, suffering and solitude.

"Yet in spite of my fault-finding I love my children, as I call them, for all are not butterflies. Many find wealth no temptation to forgetfulness of duty or hardness of heart. Many give freely of their abundance, pity the poor, comfort the afflicted, and make our city loved and honored in other lands as in our own. They have their cares, losses, and heartaches as well as the poor; it isn't all sunshine with them, and they learn, poor souls, that

'Into each life some rain must fall,

Some days must be dark and dreary.'

"But I've hopes of them, and lately they have had a teacher so genial, so gifted, so well-beloved that all who listen to him must be better for the lessons of charity, good-will and cheerfulness which he brings home to them by the magic of tears and smiles.

We know him, we love him, we always remember him as the year comes round, and the blithest song our brazen tongues utter is a Christmas carol to the Father of 'The Chimes!'"

As the spirit spoke his voice grew cheery, his old face shone, and in a burst of hearty enthusiasm he flung up his cap and cheered like a boy. So did the others, and as the fairy shout echoed through the belfry a troop of shadowy figures, with faces lovely or grotesque, tragical or gay, sailed by on the wings of the wintry wind and waved their hands to the spirits of the bells.

As the excitement subsided and the spirits reseated themselves, looking ten years younger for that burst, another spoke. A venerable brother in a dingy mantle, with a tuneful voice, and eyes that seemed to have grown sad with looking on much misery.

"He loves the poor, the man we've just hurrahed for, and he makes others love and remember them, bless him!" said the spirit. "I hope he'll touch the hearts of those who listen to him here and beguile them to open their hands to my unhappy children over yonder. If I could set some of the forlorn souls in my parish beside the happier creatures who weep over imaginary woes as they are painted by his eloquent lips, that brilliant scene would be better than any sermon. Day and night I look down on lives as full of sin, self-sacrifice and suffering as any in those famous books. Day and night I try to comfort the poor by my cheery voice, and to make their wants known by proclaiming them with all my might. But people seem to be so intent on business, pleasure or home duties that they have no time to hear and answer my appeal. There's a deal of charity in this good city, and when the people do wake up they work with a will; but I can't help thinking that if some of the money lavished on luxuries was spent on necessaries for the poor, there would be fewer tragedies like that which ended yesterday. It's a short story, easy to tell, though long and hard to live; listen to it.

"Down yonder in the garret of one of the squalid houses at the foot of my tower, a little girl has lived for a year, fighting silently and single-handed a good fight against poverty and sin. I saw her when she first came, a hopeful, cheerful, brave-hearted little soul, alone, yet not afraid. She used to sit all day sewing at her window, and her lamp burnt far into the night, for she was very poor, and all she earned would barely give her food and shelter. I watched her feed the doves, who seemed to be her only friends; she never forgot them, and daily gave them the few crumbs that fell from her meagre table. But there was no kind hand to feed and foster the little human dove, and so she starved.

"For a while she worked bravely, but the poor three dollars a week would not clothe and feed and warm her, though the things her busy fingers made sold for enough to keep her comfortably if she had received it. I saw the pretty color fade from her cheeks; her eyes grew hollow, her voice lost its cheery ring, her step its elasticity, and her face began to wear the haggard, anxious look that made its youth doubly pathetic. Her poor little gowns grew shabby, her shawl so thin she shivered when the pitiless wind smote her, and her feet were almost bare. Rain and snow beat on the patient little figure going to and fro, each morning with hope and courage faintly shining, each evening with the shadow of despair gathering darker round her. It was a hard time for all, desperately hard for her, and in her poverty, sin and pleasure tempted her. She resisted, but as another bitter winter came she feared that in her misery she might yield, for body and soul were weakened now by the long struggle. She knew not where to turn for help; there seemed to be no place for her at any safe and happy fireside; life's hard aspect daunted her, and she turned to death, saying confidingly, 'Take me while I'm innocent and not afraid to go.'

"I saw it all! I saw how she sold everything that would bring money and paid her little debts to the utmost penny; how she set her poor room in order for the last time; how she tenderly bade the doves good-by, and lay down on her bed to die. At nine o'clock last night as my bell rang over the city, I tried to tell what was going on in the garret where the light was dying out so fast. I cried to them with all my strength,—

"'Kind souls, below there! a fellow-creature is perishing for lack of charity! Oh, help her before it is too late! Mothers, with little daughters on your knees, stretch out your hands and take her in! Happy women, in the safe shelter of home, think of her desolation! Rich men, who grind the faces of the poor, remember that this soul will one day be required of you! Dear Lord, let not this little sparrow fall to the ground! Help, Christian men and women, in the name of Him whose birthday blessed the world!'

"Ah me! I rang, and clashed, and cried in vain. The passers-by only said, as they hurried home, laden with Christmas cheer: 'The old bell is merry to-night, as it should be at this blithe season, bless it!'

"As the clocks struck ten, the poor child lay down, saying, as she drank the last bitter draught life could give her, 'It's very cold, but soon I shall not feel it;' and with her quiet eyes fixed on the cross that glimmered in the moonlight above me, she lay waiting for the sleep that needs no lullaby.

"As the clock struck eleven, pain and poverty for her were over. It was bitter cold, but she no longer felt it. She lay serenely sleeping, with tired heart and hands, at rest forever. As the clocks struck twelve, the dear Lord remembered her, and with fatherly hand led her into the home where there is room for all. To-day I rung her knell, and though my heart was heavy, yet my soul was glad; for in spite of all her human woe and weakness, I am sure that little girl will keep a joyful Christmas up in heaven."

In the silence which the spirits for a moment kept, a breath of softer air than any from the snowy world below swept through the steeple and seemed to whisper, "Yes!"

"Avast there! fond as I am of salt water, I don't like this kind," cried the breezy voice of the fourth spirit, who had a tiny ship instead of a tassel on his cap, and who wiped his wet eyes with the sleeve of his rough blue cloak. "It won't take me long to spin my yarn; for things are pretty taut and ship-shape aboard our craft. Captain Taylor is an experienced sailor, and has brought many a ship safely into port in spite of wind and tide, and the devil's own whirlpools and hurricanes. If you want to see earnestness come aboard some Sunday when the Captain's on the quarter-deck, and take an observation. No danger of falling asleep there, no more than there is up aloft, 'when the stormy winds do blow.' Consciences get raked fore and aft, sins are blown clean out of the water, false colors are hauled down and true ones run up to the masthead, and many an immortal soul is warned to steer off in time from the pirates, rocks and quicksands of temptation. He's a regular revolving light, is the Captain,—a beacon always burning and saying plainly, 'Here are life-boats, ready to put off in all weathers and bring the shipwrecked into quiet waters.' He comes but seldom now, being laid up in the home dock, tranquilly waiting till his turn comes to go out with the tide and safely ride at anchor in the great harbor of the Lord. Our crew varies a good deal. Some of 'em have rather rough voyages, and come into port pretty well battered; land-sharks full foul of a good many, and do a deal of damage; but most of 'em carry brave and tender hearts under the blue jackets, for their rough nurse, the sea, manages to keep something of the child alive in the grayest old tar that makes the world his picture-book. We try to supply 'em with life-preservers while at sea, and make 'em feel sure of a hearty welcome when ashore, and I believe the year '67 will sail away into eternity with a satisfactory cargo. Brother North-End made me pipe my eye; so I'll make him laugh to pay for it, by telling a clerical joke I heard the other day. Bell-ows didn't make it, though he might have done so, as he's a connection of ours, and knows how to use his tongue as well as any of us. Speaking of the bells of a certain town, a reverend gentleman affirmed that each bell uttered an appropriate remark so plainly, that the words were audible to all. The Baptist bell cried, briskly, 'Come up and be dipped! come up and be dipped!' The Episcopal bell slowly said, 'Apos-tol-ic suc-cess-ion! apos-tol-ic suc-cess-ion!' The Orthodox bell solemnly pronounced, 'Eternal damnation! eternal damnation!' and the Methodist shouted, invitingly, 'Room for all! room for all!'"

As the spirit imitated the various calls, as only a jovial bell-sprite could, the others gave him a chime of laughter, and vowed they would each adopt some tune-ful summons, which should reach human ears and draw human feet more willingly to church.

"Faith, brother, you've kept your word and got the laugh out of us," cried a stout, sleek spirit, with a kindly face, and a row of little saints round his cap and a rosary at his side. “It’s very well we are doing this year; the cathedral is full, the flock increasing, and the true faith holding its own entirely. Ye may shake your heads if you will and fear there’ll be trouble, but I doubt it. We’ve warm hearts of our own, and the best of us don’t forget that when we were starving, America—the saints bless the jewel!—sent us bread; when we were dying for lack of work, America opened her arms and took us in, and now helps us to build churches, homes and schools by giving us a share of the riches all men work for and win. It’s a generous nation ye are, and a brave one, and we showed our gratitude by fighting for ye in the day of trouble and giving ye our Phil, and many another broth of a boy. The land is wide enough for us both, and while we work and fight and grow together, each may learn something from the other. I’m free to confess that your religion looks a bit cold and hard to me, even here in the good city where each man may ride his own hobby to death, and hoot at his neighbors as much as he will. You seem to keep your piety shut up all the week in your bare, white churches, and only let it out on Sundays, just a trifle musty with disuse. You set your rich, warm and soft to the fore, and leave the poor shivering at the door. You give your people bare walls to look upon, commonplace music to listen to, dull sermons to put them asleep, and then wonder why they stay away, or take no interest when they come.

“We leave our doors open day and night; our lamps are always burning, and we may come into our Father’s house at any hour. We let rich and poor kneel together, all being equal there. With us abroad you’ll see prince and peasant side by side, school-boy and bishop, market-woman and noble lady, saint and sinner, praying to the Holy Mary, whose motherly arms are open to high and low. We make our churches inviting with immortal music, pictures by the world's great masters, and rites that are splendid symbols of the faith we hold. Call it mummery if ye like, but let me ask you why so many of your sheep stray into our fold? It's because they miss the warmth, the hearty, the maternal tenderness which all souls love and long for, and fail to find in your stern, Puritanical belief. By Saint Peter! I've seen many a lukewarm worshipper, who for years has nodded in your cushioned pews, wake and glow with something akin to genuine piety while kneeling on the stone pavement of one of our cathedrals, with Raphael's angels before his eyes, with strains of magnificent music in his ears, and all about him, in shapes of power or beauty, the saints and martyrs who have saved the world, and whose presence inspires him to follow their divine example. It's not complaining of ye I am, but just reminding ye that men are but children after all, and need more tempting to virtue than they do to vice, which last comes easy to 'em since the Fall. Do your best in your own ways to get the poor souls into bliss, and good luck to ye. But remember, there's room in the Holy Mother Church for all, and when your own priests send ye to the divil, come straight to us and we'll take ye in."

"A truly Catholic welcome, bull and all," said the sixth spirit, who, in spite of his old-fashioned garments, had a youthful face, earnest, fearless eyes, and an energetic voice that woke the echoes with its vigorous tones. "I've a hopeful report, brothers, for the reforms of the day are wheeling into rank and marching on. The war isn't over nor rebeldom conquered yet, but the Old Guard has been 'up and at 'em' through the year. There has been some hard fighting, rivers of ink have flowed, and the Washington dawdlers have signalized themselves by a 'masterly inactivity.' The political campaign has been an anxious one; some of the leaders have deserted; some been mustered out; some have fallen gallantly, and as yet have received no monuments. But at the Grand Review the Cross of the Legion of Honor will surely shine on many a brave breast that won no decoration but its virtue here; for the world's fanatics make heaven's heroes, poets say.

"The flock of Nightingales that flew South during the 'winter of our discontent' are all at home again, some here and some in Heaven. But the music of their womanly heroism still lingers in the nation's memory, and makes a tender minor-chord in the battle-hymn of freedom.

"The reform in literature isn't as vigorous as I could wish; but a sharp attack of mental and moral dyspepsia will soon teach our people that French confectionery and the bad pastry of Wood, Braddon, Yates & Co. is not the best diet for the rising generation.

"Speaking of the rising generation reminds me of the schools. They are doing well; they always are, and we are justly proud of them. There may be a slight tendency toward placing too much value upon book-learning; too little upon home culture. Our girls are acknowledged to be uncommonly pretty, witty and wise, but some of us wish they had more health and less excitement, more domestic accomplishments and fewer ologies and isms, and were contented with simple pleasures and the old-fashioned virtues, and not quite so fond of the fast, frivolous life that makes them old so soon. I am fond of our girls and boys. I love to ring for their christenings and marriages, to toll proudly for the brave lads in blue, and tenderly for the innocent creatures whose seats are empty under my old roof. I want to see them anxious to make Young America a model of virtue, strength and beauty, and I believe they will in time.

"There have been some important revivals in religion; for the world won't stand still, and we must keep pace or be left behind to fossilize. A free nation must have a religion broad enough to embrace all mankind, deep enough to fathom and fill the human soul, high enough to reach the source of all love and wisdom, and pure enough to satisfy the wisest and the best. Alarm bells have been rung, anathemas pronounced, and Christians, forgetful of their creed, have abused one another heartily. But the truth always triumphs in the end, and whoever sincerely believes, works and waits for it, by whatever name he calls it, will surely find his own faith blessed to him in proportion to his charity for the faith of others.

"But look!—the first red streaks of dawn are in the East. Our vigil is over, and we must fly home to welcome in the holidays. Before we part, join with me, brothers, in resolving that through the coming year we will with all our hearts and tongues,—

'Ring out the old, ring in the
new,

Ring out the false, ring in the
true;

Ring in the valiant man and free,

Ring in the Christ that is to be.'"

Then hand in hand the spirits of the bells floated away, singing in the hush of dawn the sweet song the stars sung over Bethlehem,—"Peace on earth, good will to men."

Tilly's Christmas

by Louisa May Alcott (1870)

"I'm so glad to-morrow is Christmas, because I'm going to have lots of presents."

"So am I glad, though I don't expect any presents but a pair of mittens."

"And so am I; but I shan't have any presents at all."

As the three little girls trudged home from school they said these things, and as Tilly spoke, both the others looked at her with pity and some surprise, for she spoke cheerfully, and they wondered how she could be happy when she was so poor she could have no presents on Christmas.

"Don't you wish you could find a purse full of money right here in the path?" said Kate, the child who was going to have "lots of presents."

"Oh, don't I, if I could keep it honestly!" and Tilly's eyes shone at the very thought.

"What would you buy?" asked Bessy, rubbing her cold hands, and longing for her mittens.

"I'd buy a pair of large, warm blankets, a load of wood, a shawl for mother, and a pair of shoes for me; and if there was enough left, I'd give Bessy a new hat, and then she needn't wear Ben's old felt one," answered Tilly.

The girls laughed at that; but Bessy pulled the funny hat over her ears, and said she was much obliged but she'd rather have candy.

"Let's look, and maybe we can find a purse. People are always going about with money at Christmas time, and some one may lose it here," said Kate.

So, as they went along the snowy road, they looked about them, half in earnest, half in fun. Suddenly Tilly sprang forward, exclaiming,—

"I see it! I've found it!"

The others followed, but all stopped disappointed; for it wasn't a purse, it was only a little bird. It lay upon the snow with its wings spread and feebly fluttering, as if too weak to fly. Its little feet were benumbed with cold; its once bright eyes were dull with pain, and instead of a blithe song, it could only utter a faint chirp, now and then, as if crying for help.

"Nothing but a stupid old robin; how provoking!" cried Kate, sitting down to rest.

"I shan't touch it. I found one once, and took care of it, and the ungrateful thing flew away the minute it was well," said Bessy, creeping under Kate's shawl, and putting her hands under her chin to warm them.

"Poor little birdie! How pitiful he looks, and how glad he must be to see some one coming to help him! I'll take him up gently, and carry him home to mother. Don't be frightened, dear, I'm your friend;" and Tilly knelt down in the snow, stretching her hand to the bird, with the tenderest pity in her face.

Kate and Bessy laughed.

"Don't stop for that thing; it's getting late and cold: let's go on and look for the purse," they said moving away.

"You wouldn't leave it to die!" cried Tilly. "I'd rather have the bird than the money, so I shan't look any more. The purse wouldn't be mine, and I should only be tempted to keep it; but this poor thing will thank and love me, and I'm so glad I came in time."

Gently lifting the bird, Tilly felt its tiny cold claws cling to her hand, and saw its dim eyes brighten as it nestled down with a grateful chirp.

"Now I've got a Christmas present after all," she said, smiling, as they walked on. "I always wanted a bird, and this one will be such a pretty pet for me."

"He'll fly away the first chance he gets, and die anyhow; so you'd better not waste your time over him," said Bessy.

"He can't pay you for taking care of him, and my mother says it isn't worth while to help folks that can't help us," added Kate.

"My mother says, "Do as you'd be done by;" and I'm sure I'd like any one to help me if I was dying of cold and hunger. "Love your neighbour as yourself," is another of her sayings. This bird is my little neighbour, and I'll love him and care for him, as

I often wish our rich neighbour would love and care for us," answered Tilly, breathing her warm breath over the benumbed bird, who looked up at her with confiding eyes, quick to feel and know a friend.

"What a funny girl you are," said Kate; "caring for that silly bird, and talking about loving your neighbour in that sober way. Mr. King don't care a bit for you, and never will, though he knows how poor you are; so I don't think your plan amounts to much."

"I believe it, though; and shall do my part, any way. Good-night. I hope you'll have a merry Christmas, and lots of pretty things," answered Tilly, as they parted.

Her eyes were full, and she felt so poor as she went on alone toward the little old house where she lived. It would have been so pleasant to know that she was going to have some of the pretty things all children love to find in their full stockings on Christmas morning. And pleasanter still to have been able to give her mother something nice. So many comforts were needed, and there was no hope of getting them; for they could barely get food and fire.

"Never mind, birdie, we'll make the best of what we have, and be merry in spite of every thing. You shall have a happy Christmas, any way; and I know God won't forget us if every one else does."

She stopped a minute to wipe her eyes, and lean her cheek against the bird's soft breast, finding great comfort in the little creature, though it could only love her, nothing more.

"See, mother, what a nice present I've found," she cried, going in with a cheery face that was like sunshine in the dark room.

"I'm glad of that, dearie; for I haven't been able to get my little girl anything but a rosy apple. Poor bird! Give it some of your warm bread and milk."

"Why, mother, what a big bowlful! I'm afraid you gave me all the milk," said Tilly, smiling over the nice, steaming supper that stood ready for her.

"I've had plenty, dear. Sit down and dry your wet feet, and put the bird in my basket on this warm flannel."

Tilly peeped into the closet and saw nothing there but dry bread.

"Mother's given me all the milk, and is going without her tea, 'cause she knows I'm hungry. Now I'll surprise her, and she shall have a good supper too. She is going to split wood, and I'll fix it while she's gone."

So Tilly put down the old tea-pot, carefully poured out a part of the milk, and from her pocket produced a great, plummy bun, that one of the school-children had given her, and she had saved for her mother. A slice of the dry bread was nicely toasted, and the bit of butter set by for her put on it. When her mother came in there was the table drawn up in a warm place, a hot cup of tea ready, and Tilly and birdie waiting for her.

Such a poor little supper, and yet such a happy one; for love, charity, and contentment were guests there, and that Christmas eve was a blither one than that up at the great house, where lights shone, fires blazed, a great tree glittered, and music sounded, as the children danced and played.

"We must go to bed early, for we've only wood enough to last over to-morrow. I shall be paid for my work the day after, and then we can get some," said Tilly's mother, as they sat by the fire.

"If my bird was only a fairy bird, and would give us three wishes, how nice it would be! Poor dear, he can't give me any thing; but it's no matter," answered Tilly, looking at the robin, who lay in the basket with his head under his wing, a mere little feathery bunch.

"He can give you one thing, Tilly,—the pleasure of doing good. That is one of the sweetest things in life; and the poor can enjoy it as well as the rich."

As her mother spoke, with her tired hand softly stroking her little daughter's hair, Tilly suddenly started and pointed to the window, saying, in a frightened whisper,—

"I saw a face,—a man's face, looking in! It's gone now; but I truly saw it."

"Some traveller attracted by the light perhaps. I'll go and see." And Tilly's mother went to the door.

No one was there. The wind blew cold, the stars shone, the snow lay white on field and wood, and the Christmas moon was glittering in the sky.

"What sort of a face was it?" asked Tilly's mother, coming back.

"A pleasant sort of face, I think; but I was so startled I don't quite know what it was like. I wish we had a curtain there," said Tilly.

"I like to have our light shine out in the evening, for the road is dark and lonely just here, and the twinkle of our lamp is pleasant to people's eyes as they go by. We can do so little for our neighbours, I am glad to cheer the way for them. Now put these poor old shoes to dry, and go to bed, dearie; I'll come soon."

Tilly went, taking her bird with her to sleep in his basket near by, lest he should be lonely in the night.

Soon the little house was dark and still, and no one saw the Christmas spirits at their work that night.

When Tilly opened the door next morning, she gave a loud cry, clapped her hands, and then stood still; quite speechless with wonder and delight. There, before the door, lay a great pile of wood, all ready to burn, a big bundle and a basket, with a lovely nosegay of winter roses, holly, and evergreen tied to the handle.

"Oh, mother! did the fairies do it?" cried Tilly, pale with her happiness, as she seized the basket, while her mother took in the bundle.

"Yes, dear, the best and dearest fairy in the world, called "Charity." She walks abroad at Christmas time, does beautiful deeds like this, and does not stay to be thanked," answered her mother with full eyes, as she undid the parcel.

There they were,—the warm, thick blankets, the comfortable shawls, the new shoes, and, best of all, a pretty winter hat for Bessy. The basket was full of good things to eat, and on the flowers lay a paper, saying,—

"For the little girl who loves her neighbour as herself."

"Mother, I really think my bird is a fairy bird, and all these splendid things come from him," said Tilly, laughing and crying with joy.

It really did seem so, for as she spoke, the robin flew to the table, hopped to the nosegay, and perching among the roses, began to chirp with all his little might. The sun streamed in on flowers, bird, and happy child, and no one saw a shadow glide away from the window; no one ever knew that Mr. King had seen and heard the little girls the night before, or dreamed that the rich neighbour had learned a lesson from the poor neighbour.

And Tilly's bird was a fairy bird; for by her love and tenderness to the helpless thing, she brought good gifts to herself, happiness to the unknown giver of them, and a faithful little friend who did not fly away, but stayed with her till the snow was gone, making summer for her in the winter-time.

A Christmas Dream, and How it Came True

by Louisa May Alcott (1886)

"I'm so tired of Christmas I wish there never would be another one!" exclaimed a discontented-looking little girl, as she sat idly watching her mother arrange a pile of gifts two days before they were to be given.

"Why, Effie, what a dreadful thing to say! You are as bad as old Scrooge; and I'm afraid something will happen to you, as it did to him, if you don't care for dear Christmas," answered mamma, almost dropping the silver horn she was filling with delicious candies.

"Who was Scrooge? What happened to him?" asked Effie, with a glimmer of interest in her listless face, as she picked out the sourest lemon-drop she could find; for nothing sweet suited her just then.

"He was one of Dickens's best people, and you can read the charming story some day. He hated Christmas until a strange dream showed him how dear and beautiful it was, and made a better man of him."

"I shall read it; for I like dreams, and have a great many curious ones myself. But they don't keep me from being tired of Christmas," said Effie, poking discontentedly among the sweeties for something worth eating.

"Why are you tired of what should be the happiest time of all the year?" asked mamma, anxiously.

"Perhaps I shouldn't be if I had something new. But it is always the same, and there isn't any more surprise about it. I always find heaps of goodies in my stocking. Don't like some of them, and soon get tired of those I do like. We always have a great dinner, and I eat too much, and feel ill next day. Then there is a Christmas tree somewhere, with a doll on top, or a stupid old Santa Claus, and children dancing and screaming over bonbons and toys that break, and shiny things that are of no use. Really, mamma, I've had so many Christmases all alike that I don't think I *can* bear another one." And Effie laid herself flat on the sofa, as if the mere idea was too much for her.

Her mother laughed at her despair, but was sorry to see her little girl so discontented, when she had everything to make her happy, and had known but ten Christmas days.

"Suppose we don't give you *any* presents at all,--how would that suit you?" asked mamma, anxious to please her spoiled child.

"I should like one large and splendid one, and one dear little one, to remember some very nice person by," said Effie, who was a fanciful little body, full of odd whims and notions, which her friends loved to gratify, regardless of time, trouble, or money;

for she was the last of three little girls, and very dear to all the family.

"Well, my darling, I will see what I can do to please you, and not say a word until all is ready. If I could only get a new idea to start with!" And mamma went on tying up her pretty bundles with a thoughtful face, while Effie strolled to the window to watch the rain that kept her in-doors and made her dismal.

"Seems to me poor children have better times than rich ones. I can't go out, and there is a girl about my age splashing along, without any maid to fuss about rubbers and cloaks and umbrellas and colds. I wish I was a beggar-girl."

"Would you like to be hungry, cold, and ragged, to beg all day, and sleep on an ash-heap at night?" asked mamma, wondering what would come next.

"Cinderella did, and had a nice time in the end. This girl out here has a basket of scraps on her arm, and a big old shawl all round her, and doesn't seem to care a bit, though the water runs out of the toes of her boots. She goes paddling along, laughing at the rain, and eating a cold potato as if it tasted nicer than the chicken and ice-cream I had for dinner. Yes, I do think poor children are happier than rich ones."

"So do I, sometimes. At the Orphan Asylum today I saw two dozen merry little souls who have no parents, no home, and no hope of Christmas beyond a stick of candy or a cake. I wish you had been there to see how happy they were, playing with the old toys some richer children had sent them."

"You may give them all mine; I'm so tired of them I never want to see them again," said Effie, turning from the window to the pretty baby-house full of everything a child's heart could desire.

"I will, and let you begin again with something you will not tire of, if I can only find it." And mamma knit her brows trying to discover some grand surprise for this child who didn't care for Christmas.

Nothing more was said then; and wandering off to the library, Effie found "A Christmas Carol," and curling herself up in the sofa corner, read it all before tea. Some of it she did not understand; but she laughed and cried over many parts of the charming story, and felt better without knowing why.

All the evening she thought of poor Tiny Tim, Mrs. Cratchit with the pudding, and the stout old gentleman who danced so gayly that "his legs twinkled in the air." Presently bedtime arrived.

"Come, now, and toast your feet," said Effie's nurse, "while I do your pretty hair and tell stories."

"I'll have a fairy tale to-night, a very interesting one," commanded Effie, as she put on her blue silk wrapper and little fur-lined slippers to sit before the fire and have her long curls brushed.

So Nursey told her best tales; and when at last the child lay down under her lace curtains, her head was full of a curious jumble of Christmas elves, poor children, snow-storms, sugarplums, and surprises. So it is no wonder that she dreamed all night; and this was the dream, which she never quite forgot.

She found herself sitting on a stone, in the middle of a great field, all alone. The snow was falling fast, a bitter wind whistled by, and night was coming on. She felt hungry, cold, and tired, and did not know where to go nor what to do.

"I wanted to be a beggar-girl, and now I am one; but I don't like it, and wish somebody would come and take care of me. I don't know who I am, and I think I must be lost," thought Effie, with the curious interest one takes in one's self in dreams.

But the more she thought about it, the more bewildered she felt. Faster fell the snow, colder blew the wind, darker grew the night; and poor Effie made up her mind that she was quite forgotten and left to freeze alone. The tears were chilled on her cheeks, her feet felt like icicles, and her heart died within her, so hungry, frightened, and forlorn was she. Laying her head on her knees, she gave herself up for lost, and sat there with the great flakes fast turning her to a little white mound, when suddenly the sound of music reached her, and starting up, she looked and listened with all her eyes and ears.

Far away a dim light shone, and a voice was heard singing. She tried to run toward the welcome glimmer, but could not stir, and stood like a small statue of expectation while the light drew nearer, and the sweet words of the song grew clearer.

From our happy home
Through the world we roam
One week in all the year,
Making winter spring
With the joy we bring,
For Christmas-tide is here.

Now the eastern star
Shines from afar
To light the poorest home;
Hearts warmer grow,
Gifts freely flow,
For Christmas-tide has come.

Now gay trees rise
Before young eyes,
Abloom with tempting cheer;
Blithe voices sing,
And blithe bells ring,
For Christmas-tide is here.

Oh, happy chime,
Oh, blessed time,
That draws us all so near!
"Welcome, dear day,"
All creatures say,
For Christmas-tide is here.

A child's voice sang, a child's hand carried the little candle; and in the circle of soft light it shed, Effie saw a pretty child coming to her through the night and snow. A rosy, smiling creature, wrapped in white fur, with a wreath of green and scarlet holly on its shining hair, the magic candle in one hand, and the other outstretched as if to shower gifts and warmly press all other hands.

Effie forgot to speak as this bright vision came nearer, leaving no trace of footsteps in the snow, only lighting the way with its little candle, and filling the air with the music of its song.

"Dear child, you are lost, and I have come to find you," said the stranger, taking Effie's cold hands in his, with a smile like sunshine, while every holly berry glowed like a little fire.

"Do you know me?" asked Effie, feeling no fear, but a great gladness, at his coming.

"I know all children, and go to find them; for this is my holiday, and I gather them from all parts of the world to be merry with me once a year."

"Are you an angel?" asked Effie, looking for the wings.

"No; I am a Christmas spirit, and live with my mates in a pleasant place, getting ready for our holiday, when we are let out to roam about the world, helping make this a happy time for all who will let us in. Will you come and see how we work?"

"I will go anywhere with you. Don't leave me again," cried Effie, gladly.

"First I will make you comfortable. That is what we love to do. You are cold, and you shall be warm, hungry, and I will feed you; sorrowful, and I will make you gay."

With a wave of his candle all three miracles were wrought,--for the snow- flakes turned to a white fur cloak and hood on Effie's head and shoulders, a bowl of hot soup came sailing to her lips, and vanished when she had eagerly drunk the last drop; and suddenly the dismal field changed to a new world so full of wonders that all her troubles were forgotten in a minute.

Bells were ringing so merrily that it was hard to keep from dancing. Green garlands hung on the walls, and every tree was a Christmas tree full of toys, and blazing with candles that never went out.

In one place many little spirits sewed like mad on warm clothes, turning off work faster than any sewing-machine ever invented, and great piles were made ready to be sent to poor people. Other busy creatures packed money into purses, and wrote checks which they sent flying away on the wind,--a lovely kind of snow-storm to fall into a world below full of poverty.

Older and graver spirits were looking over piles of little books, in which the records of the past year were kept, telling how different people had spent it, and what sort of gifts they deserved. Some got peace, some disappointment, some remorse and sorrow, some great joy and hope. The rich had generous thoughts sent them; the poor, gratitude and contentment. Children had more love and duty to parents; and parents renewed patience, wisdom, and satisfaction for and in their children. No one was forgotten.

"Please tell me what splendid place this is?" asked Effie, as soon as she could collect her wits after the first look at all these astonishing things.

"This is the Christmas world; and here we work all the year round, never tired of getting ready for the happy day. See, these are the saints just setting off; for some have far to go, and the children must not be disappointed."

As he spoke the spirit pointed to four gates, out of which four great sleighs were just driving, laden with toys, while a jolly old

Santa Claus sat in the middle of each, drawing on his mittens and tucking up his wraps for a long cold drive.

"Why, I thought there was only one Santa Claus, and even he was a humbug," cried Effie, astonished at the sight.

"Never give up your faith in the sweet old stones, even after you come to see that they are only the pleasant shadow of a lovely truth."

Just then the sleighs went off with a great jingling of bells and pattering of reindeer hoofs, while all the spirits gave a cheer that was heard in the lower world, where people said, "Hear the stars sing."

"I never will say there isn't any Santa Claus again. Now, show me more."

"You will like to see this place, I think, and may learn something here perhaps."

The spirit smiled as he led the way to a little door, through which Effie peeped into a world of dolls. Baby-houses were in full blast, with dolls of all sorts going on like live people. Waxen ladies sat in their parlors elegantly dressed; black dolls cooked in the kitchens; nurses walked out with the bits of dollies; and the streets were full of tin soldiers marching, wooden horses prancing, express wagons rumbling, and little men hurrying to and fro. Shops were there, and tiny people buying legs of mutton, pounds of tea, mites of clothes, and everything dolls use or wear or want.

But presently she saw that in some ways the dolls improved upon the manners and customs of human beings, and she watched eagerly to learn why they did these things. A fine Paris doll driving in her carriage took up a black worsted Dinah who was hobbling along with a basket of clean clothes, and carried her to her journey's end, as if it were the proper thing to do. Another interesting china lady took off her comfortable red cloak and put it round a poor wooden creature done up in a paper shift, and so badly painted that its face would have sent some babies into fits.

"Seems to me I once knew a rich girl who didn't give her things to poor girls. I wish I could remember who she was, and tell her to be as kind as that china doll," said Effie, much touched at the sweet way the pretty creature wrapped up the poor fright, and then ran off in her little gray gown to buy a shiny fowl stuck on a wooden platter for her invalid mother's dinner.

"We recall these things to people's minds by dreams. I think the girl you speak of won't forget this one." And the spirit smiled, as if he enjoyed some joke which she did not see.

A little bell rang as she looked, and away scampered the children into the red-and-green school-house with the roof that lifted up, so one could see how nicely they sat at their desks with mites of books, or drew on the inch-square blackboards with crumbs of chalk.

"They know their lessons very well, and are as still as mice. We make a great racket at our school, and get bad marks every day. I shall tell the girls they had better mind what they do, or their dolls will be better scholars than they are," said Effie, much impressed, as she peeped in and saw no rod in the hand of the little mistress, who looked up and shook her head at the intruder, as if begging her to go away before the order of the school was disturbed.

Effie retired at once, but could not resist one look in at the window of a fine mansion, where the family were at dinner, the children behaved so well at table, and never grumbled a bit when their mamma said they could not have any more fruit.

"Now, show me something else," she said, as they came again to the low door that led out of Doll-land.

"You have seen how we prepare for Christmas; let me show you where we love best to send our good and happy gifts," answered the spirit, giving her his hand again.

"I know. I've seen ever so many," began Effie, thinking of her own Christmases.

"No, you have never seen what I will show you. Come away, and remember what you see to-night."

Like a flash that bright world vanished, and Effie found herself in a part of the city she had never seen before. It was far away from the gayer places, where every store was brilliant with lights and full of pretty things, and every house wore a festival air, while people hurried to and fro with merry greetings. It was down among the dingy streets where the poor lived, and where there was no making ready for Christmas.

Hungry women looked in at the shabby shops, longing to buy meat and bread, but empty pockets forbade. Tipsy men drank up their wages in the bar- rooms; and in many cold dark chambers little children huddled under the thin blankets, trying to forget their misery in sleep.

No nice dinners filled the air with savory smells, no gay trees dropped toys and bonbons into eager hands, no little stockings hung in rows beside the chimney-piece ready to be filled, no happy sounds of music, gay voices, and dancing feet were heard; and there were no signs of Christmas anywhere.

"Don't they have any in this place?" asked Effie, shivering, as she held fast the spirit's hand, following where he led her.

"We come to bring it. Let me show you our best workers." And the spirit pointed to some sweet-faced men and women who came stealing into the poor houses, working such beautiful miracles that Effie could only stand and watch.

Some slipped money into the empty pockets, and sent the happy mothers to buy all the comforts they needed; others led the drunken men out of temptation, and took them home to find safer pleasures there. Fires were kindled on cold hearths, tables spread as if by magic, and warm clothes wrapped round shivering limbs. Flowers suddenly bloomed in the chambers of the sick; old people found themselves remembered; sad hearts were consoled by a tender word, and wicked ones softened by the story of Him who forgave all sin.

But the sweetest work was for the children; and Effie held her breath to watch these human fairies hang up and fill the little stockings without which a child's Christmas is not perfect, putting in things that once she would have thought very humble presents, but which now seemed beautiful and precious because these poor babies had nothing.

"That is so beautiful! I wish I could make merry Christmases as these good people do, and be loved and thanked as they are," said Effie, softly, as she watched the busy men and women do their work and steal away without thinking of any reward but their own satisfaction.

"You can if you will. I have shown you the way. Try it, and see how happy your own holiday will be hereafter."

As he spoke, the spirit seemed to put his arms about her, and vanished with a kiss.

"Oh, stay and show me more!" cried Effie, trying to hold him fast.

"Darling, wake up, and tell me why you are smiling in your sleep," said a voice in her ear; and opening her eyes, there was mamma bending over her, and morning sunshine streaming into the room.

"Are they all gone? Did you hear the bells? Wasn't it splendid?" she asked, rubbing her eyes, and looking about her for the pretty child who was so real and sweet.

"You have been dreaming at a great rate,--talking in your sleep, laughing, and clapping your hands as if you were cheering some one. Tell me what was so splendid," said mamma, smoothing the tumbled hair and lifting up the sleepy head.

Then, while she was being dressed, Effie told her dream, and Nursey thought it very wonderful; but mamma smiled to see how curiously things the child had thought, read, heard, and seen through the day were mixed up in her sleep.

"The spirit said I could work lovely miracles if I tried; but I don't know how to begin, for I have no magic candle to make feasts appear, and light up groves of Christmas trees, as he did," said Effie, sorrowfully.

"Yes, you have. We will do it! we will do it!" And clapping her hands, mamma suddenly began to dance all over the room as if she had lost her wits.

"How? how? You must tell me, mamma," cried Effie, dancing after her, and ready to believe anything possible when she remembered the adventures of the past night.

"I've got it! I've got it!--the new idea. A splendid one, if I can only carry it out!" And mamma waltzed the little girl round till her curls flew wildly in the air, while Nursey laughed as if she would die.

"Tell me! tell me!" shrieked Effie. "No, no; it is a surprise,--a grand surprise for Christmas day!" sung mamma, evidently charmed with her happy thought. "Now, come to breakfast; for we must work like bees if we want to play spirits tomorrow. You and Nursey will go out shopping, and get heaps of things, while I arrange matters behind the scenes."

They were running downstairs as mamma spoke, and Effie called out breathlessly,--

"It won't be a surprise; for I know you are going to ask some poor children here, and have a tree or something. It won't be like my dream; for they had ever so many trees, and more children than we can find anywhere."

"There will be no tree, no party, no dinner, in this house at all, and no presents for you. Won't that be a surprise?" And mamma laughed at Effie's bewildered face.

"Do it. I shall like it, I think; and I won't ask any questions, so it will all burst upon me when the time comes," she said; and she ate her breakfast thoughtfully, for this really would be a new sort of Christmas.

All that morning Effie trotted after Nursey in and out of shops, buying dozens of barking dogs, woolly lambs, and squeaking birds; tiny tea-sets, gay picture-books, mittens and hoods, dolls and candy. Parcel after parcel was sent home; but when Effie returned she saw no trace of them, though she peeped everywhere. Nursey chuckled, but wouldn't give a hint, and went out again in the afternoon with a long list of more things to buy; while Effie wandered forlornly about the house, missing the usual merry stir that went before the Christmas dinner and the evening fun.

As for mamma, she was quite invisible all day, and came in at night so tired that she could only lie on the sofa to rest, smiling as if some very pleasant thought made her happy in spite of weariness.

"Is the surprise going on all right?" asked Effie, anxiously; for it seemed an immense time to wait till another evening came.

"Beautifully! better than I expected; for several of my good friends are helping, or I couldn't have done it as I wish. I know you will like it, dear, and long remember this new way of making Christmas merry."

Mamma gave her a very tender kiss, and Effie went to bed.

The next day was a very strange one; for when she woke there was no stocking to examine, no pile of gifts under her napkin, no one said "Merry Christmas!" to her, and the dinner was just as usual to her. Mamma vanished again, and Nursey kept wiping her eyes and saying: "The dear things! It's the prettiest idea I ever heard of. No one but your blessed ma could have done it."

"Do stop, Nursey, or I shall go crazy because I don't know the secret!" cried Effie, more than once; and she kept her eye on the clock, for at seven in the evening the surprise was to come off.

The longed-for hour arrived at last, and the child was too excited to ask questions when Nurse put on her cloak and hood, led her to the carriage, and they drove away, leaving their house the one dark and silent one in the row.

"I feel like the girls in the fairy tales who are led off to strange places and see fine things," said Effie, in a whisper, as they jingled through the gay streets.

"Ah, my deary, it *is* like a fairy tale, I do assure you, and you *will* see finer things than most children will tonight. Steady, now, and do just as I tell you, and don't say one word whatever you see," answered Nursey, quite quivering with excitement as she patted a large box in her lap, and nodded and laughed with twinkling eyes.

They drove into a dark yard, and Effie was led through a back door to a little room, where Nurse coolly proceeded to take off not only her cloak and hood, but her dress and shoes also. Effie stared and bit her lips, but kept still until out of the box came a little white fur coat and boots, a wreath of holly leaves and berries, and a candle with a frill of gold paper round it. A long "Oh!" escaped her then; and when she was dressed and saw herself in the glass, she started back, exclaiming, "Why, Nursey, I look like the spirit in my dream!"

"So you do; and that's the part you are to play, my pretty! Now whist, while I blind your eyes and put you in your place."

"Shall I be afraid?" whispered Effie, full of wonder; for as they went out she heard the sound of many voices, the tramp of many feet, and, in spite of the bandage, was sure a great light shone upon her when she stopped.

"You needn't be; I shall stand close by, and your ma will be there."

After the handkerchief was tied about her eyes, Nurse led Effie up some steps, and placed her on a high platform, where something like leaves touched her head, and the soft snap of lamps seemed to fill the air.

Music began as soon as Nurse clapped her hands, the voices outside sounded nearer, and the tramp was evidently coming up the stairs.

"Now, my precious, look and see how you and your dear ma have made a merry Christmas for them that needed it!"

Off went the bandage; and for a minute Effie really did think she was asleep again, for she actually stood in "a grove of Christmas trees," all gay and shining as in her vision. Twelve on a side, in two rows down the room, stood the little pines, each on its low table; and behind Effie a taller one rose to the roof, hung with wreaths of popcorn, apples, oranges, horns of candy, and cakes of all sorts, from sugary hearts to gingerbread Jumbos. On the smaller trees she saw many of her own discarded toys and those Nursey bought, as well as heaps that seemed to have rained down straight from that delightful Christmas country where she felt as if she was again.

"How splendid! Who is it for? What is that noise? Where is mamma?" cried Effie, pale with pleasure and surprise, as she stood looking down the brilliant little street from her high place.

Before Nurse could answer, the doors at the lower end flew open, and in marched twenty-four little blue-gowned orphan girls, singing sweetly, until amazement changed the song to cries of joy and wonder as the shining spectacle appeared. While they stood staring with round eyes at the wilderness of pretty things about them, mamma stepped up beside Effie, and holding her hand fast to give her courage, told the story of the dream in a few simple words, ending in this way:--

"So my little girl wanted to be a Christmas spirit too, and make this a happy day for those who had not as many pleasures and comforts as she has. She likes surprises, and we planned this for you all. She shall play the good fairy, and give each of you something from this tree, after which every one will find her own name on a small tree, and can go to enjoy it in her own way. March by, my dears, and let us fill your hands."

Nobody told them to do it, but all the hands were clapped heartily before a single child stirred; then one by one they came to look up wonderingly at the pretty giver of the feast as she leaned down to offer them great yellow oranges, red apples, bunches of grapes, bonbons, and cakes, till all were gone, and a double row of smiling faces turned toward her as the children filed back to their places in the orderly way they had been taught.

Then each was led to her own tree by the good ladies who had helped mamma with all their hearts; and the happy hubbub that arose would have satisfied even Santa Claus himself,--shrieks of joy, dances of delight, laughter and tears (for some tender little things could not bear so much pleasure at once, and sobbed with mouths full of candy and hands full of toys). How they ran to show one another the new treasures! how they peeped and tasted, pulled and pinched, until the air was full of queer noises, the floor covered with papers, and the little trees left bare of all but candles!

"I don't think heaven can be any gooder than this," sighed one small girl, as she looked about her in a blissful maze, holding her full apron with one hand, while she luxuriously carried sugar-plums to her mouth with the other.

"Is that a truly angel up there?" asked another, fascinated by the little white figure with the wreath on its shining hair, who in some mysterious way had been the cause of all this merry-making.

"I wish I dared to go and kiss her for this splendid party," said a lame child, leaning on her crutch, as she stood near the steps, wondering how it seemed to sit in a mother's lap, as Effie was doing, while she watched the happy scene before her.

Effie heard her, and remembering Tiny Tim, ran down and put her arms about the pale child, kissing the wistful face, as she said sweetly, "You may; but mamma deserves the thanks. She did it all; I only dreamed about it."

Lame Katy felt as if "a truly angel" was embracing her, and could only stammer out her thanks, while the other children ran to see the pretty spirit, and touch her soft dress, until she stood in a crowd of blue gowns laughing as they held up their gifts for her to see and admire.

Mamma leaned down and whispered one word to the older girls; and suddenly they all took hands to dance round Effie, singing as they skipped.

It was a pretty sight, and the ladies found it hard to break up the happy revel; but it was late for small people, and too much fun is a mistake. So the girls fell into line, and marched before Effie and mamma again, to say goodnight with such grateful little faces that the eyes of those who looked grew dim with tears. Mamma kissed every one; and many a hungry childish heart felt as if the touch of those tender lips was their best gift. Effie shook so many small hands that her own tingled; and when Katy came she pressed a small doll into Effie's hand, whispering, "You didn't have a single present, and we had lots. Do keep that; it's the prettiest thing I got."

"I will," answered Effie, and held it fast until the last smiling face was gone, the surprise all over, and she safe in her own bed, too tired and happy for anything but sleep.

"Mamma, it was a beautiful surprise, and I thank you so much! I don't see how you did it; but I like it best of all the Christmases I ever had, and mean to make one every year. I had my splendid big present, and here is the dear little one to keep for love of poor Katy; so even that part of my wish came true."

And Effie fell asleep with a happy smile on her lips, her one humble gift still in her hand, and a new love for Christmas in her heart that never changed through a long life spent in doing good.

A Kidnapped Santa Claus

by L. Frank Bank (1904)

Santa Claus lives in the Laughing Valley, where stands the big, rambling castle in which his toys are manufactured. His workmen, selected from the ryls, knooks, pixies and fairies, live with him, and every one is as busy as can be from one year's end to another.

It is called the Laughing Valley because everything there is happy and gay. The brook chuckles to itself as it leaps rollicking between its green banks; the wind whistles merrily in the trees; the sunbeams dance lightly over the soft grass, and the violets and wild flowers look smilingly up from their green nests. To laugh one needs to be happy; to be happy one needs to be content. And throughout the Laughing Valley of Santa Claus contentment reigns supreme.

On one side is the mighty Forest of Burzee. At the other side stands the huge mountain that contains the Caves of the Daemons. And between them the Valley lies smiling and peaceful.

One would think that our good old Santa Claus, who devotes his days to making children happy, would have no enemies on all the earth; and, as a matter of fact, for a long period of time he encountered nothing but love wherever he might go.

But the Daemons who live in the mountain caves grew to hate Santa Claus very much, and all for the simple reason that he made children happy.

The Caves of the Daemons are five in number. A broad pathway leads up to the first cave, which is a finely arched cavern at the foot of the mountain, the entrance being beautifully carved and decorated. In it resides the Daemon of Selfishness. Back of this is another cavern inhabited by the Daemon of Envy. The cave of the Daemon of Hatred is next in order, and through this one passes to the home of the Daemon of Malice -- situated in a dark and fearful cave in the very heart of the mountain. I do not know what lies beyond this. Some say there are terrible pitfalls leading to death and destruction, and this may very well be true. However, from each one of the four caves mentioned there is a small, narrow tunnel leading to the fifth cave -- a cozy little room occupied by the Daemon of Repentance. And as the rocky floors of these passages are well worn by the track of passing feet, I judge that many wanderers in the Caves of the Daemons have escaped through the tunnels to the abode of the Daemon of Repentance, who is said to be a pleasant sort of fellow who gladly opens for one a little door admitting you into fresh air and sunshine again.

Well, these Daemons of the Caves, thinking they had great cause to dislike old Santa Claus, held a meeting one day to discuss the matter.

"I'm really getting lonesome," said the Daemon of Selfishness. "For Santa Claus distributes so many pretty Christmas gifts to all the children that they become happy and generous, through his example, and keep away from my cave."

"I'm having the same trouble," rejoined the Daemon of Envy. "The little ones seem quite content with Santa Claus, and there are few, indeed, that I can coax to become envious."

"And that makes it bad for me!" declared the Daemon of Hatred. "For if no children pass through the Caves of Selfishness and Envy, none can get to MY cavern."

"Or to mine," added the Daemon of Malice.

"For my part," said the Daemon of Repentance, "it is easily seen that if children do not visit your caves they have no need to visit mine; so that I am quite as neglected as you are."

"And all because of this person they call Santa Claus!" exclaimed the Daemon of Envy. "He is simply ruining our business, and something must be done at once."

To this they readily agreed; but what to do was another and more difficult matter to settle. They knew that Santa Claus worked all through the year at his castle in the Laughing Valley, preparing the gifts he was to distribute on Christmas Eve; and at first they resolved to try to tempt him into their caves, that they might lead him on to the terrible pitfalls that ended in destruction.

So the very next day, while Santa Claus was busily at work, surrounded by his little band of assistants, the Daemon of Selfishness came to him and said:

"These toys are wonderfully bright and pretty. Why do you not keep them for yourself? It's a pity to give them to those noisy boys and fretful girls, who break and destroy them so quickly."

"Nonsense!" cried the old graybeard, his bright eyes twinkling merrily as he turned toward the tempting Daemon. "The boys and girls are never so noisy and fretful after receiving my presents, and if I can make them happy for one day in the year I am quite content."

So the Daemon went back to the others, who awaited him in their caves, and said:

"I have failed, for Santa Claus is not at all selfish."

The following day the Daemon of Envy visited Santa Claus. Said he: "The toy shops are full of playthings quite as pretty as those you are making. What a shame it is that they should interfere with your business! They make toys by machinery much quicker than you can make them by hand; and they sell them for money, while you get nothing at all for your work."

But Santa Claus refused to be envious of the toy shops.

"I can supply the little ones but once a year -- on Christmas Eve," he answered; "for the children are many, and I am but one. And as my work is one of love and kindness I would be ashamed to receive money for my little gifts. But throughout all the year the children must be amused in some way, and so the toy shops are able to bring much happiness to my little friends. I like the toy shops, and am glad to see them prosper."

In spite of the second rebuff, the Daemon of Hatred thought he would try to influence Santa Claus. So the next day he entered the busy workshop and said:

"Good morning, Santa! I have bad news for you."

"Then run away, like a good fellow," answered Santa Claus. "Bad news is something that should be kept secret and never told."

"You cannot escape this, however," declared the Daemon; "for in the world are a good many who do not believe in Santa Claus, and these you are bound to hate bitterly, since they have so wronged you."

"Stuff and rubbish!" cried Santa.

"And there are others who resent your making children happy and who sneer at you and call you a foolish old rattlepate! You are quite right to hate such base slanderers, and you ought to be revenged upon them for their evil words."

"But I don't hate 'em!" exclaimed Santa Claus positively. "Such people do me no real harm, but merely render themselves and their children unhappy. Poor things! I'd much rather help them any day than injure them."

Indeed, the Daemons could not tempt old Santa Claus in any way. On the contrary, he was shrewd enough to see that their object in visiting him was to make mischief and trouble, and his cheery laughter disconcerted the evil ones and showed to them the folly of such an undertaking. So they abandoned honeyed words and determined to use force.

It was well known that no harm can come to Santa Claus while he is in the Laughing Valley, for the fairies, and ryls, and knooks all protect him. But on Christmas Eve he drives his reindeer out into the big world, carrying a sleighload of toys and pretty gifts to the children; and this was the time and the occasion when his enemies had the best chance to injure him. So the Daemons laid their plans and awaited the arrival of Christmas Eve.

The moon shone big and white in the sky, and the snow lay crisp and sparkling on the ground as Santa Claus cracked his whip and sped away out of the Valley into the great world beyond. The roomy sleigh was packed full with huge sacks of toys, and as the reindeer dashed onward our jolly old Santa laughed and whistled and sang for very joy. For in all his merry life this was the one day in the year when he was happiest -- the day he lovingly bestowed the treasures of his workshop upon the little children.

It would be a busy night for him, he well knew. As he whistled and shouted and cracked his whip again, he reviewed in mind all the towns and cities and farmhouses where he was expected, and figured that he had just enough presents to go around and make every child happy. The reindeer knew exactly what was expected of them, and dashed along so swiftly that their feet scarcely seemed to touch the snow-covered ground.

Suddenly a strange thing happened: a rope shot through the moonlight and a big noose that was in the end of it settled over the arms and body of Santa Claus and drew tight. Before he could resist or even cry out he was jerked from the seat of the sleigh and tumbled head foremost into a snowbank, while the reindeer rushed onward with the load of toys and carried it quickly out of sight and sound.

Such a surprising experience confused old Santa for a moment, and when he had collected his senses he found that the wicked

Daemons had pulled him from the snowdrift and bound him tightly with many coils of the stout rope. And then they carried the kidnapped Santa Claus away to their mountain, where they thrust the prisoner into a secret cave and chained him to the rocky wall so that he could not escape.

"Ha, ha!" laughed the Daemons, rubbing their hands together with cruel glee. "What will the children do now? How they will cry and scold and storm when they find there are no toys in their stockings and no gifts on their Christmas trees! And what a lot of punishment they will receive from their parents, and how they will flock to our Caves of Selfishness, and Envy, and Hatred, and Malice! We have done a mighty clever thing, we Daemons of the Caves!"

Now it so chanced that on this Christmas Eve the good Santa Claus had taken with him in his sleigh Nuter the Ryl, Peter the Knook, Kilter the Pixie, and a small fairy named Wisk -- his four favorite assistants. These little people he had often found very useful in helping him to distribute his gifts to the children, and when their master was so suddenly dragged from the sleigh they were all snugly tucked underneath the seat, where the sharp wind could not reach them.

The tiny immortals knew nothing of the capture of Santa Claus until some time after he had disappeared. But finally they missed his cheery voice, and as their master always sang or whistled on his journeys, the silence warned them that something was wrong.

Little Wisk stuck out his head from underneath the seat and found Santa Claus gone and no one to direct the flight of the reindeer.

"Whoa!" he called out, and the deer obediently slackened speed and came to a halt.

Peter and Nuter and Kilter all jumped upon the seat and looked back over the track made by the sleigh. But Santa Claus had been left miles and miles behind.

"What shall we do?" asked Wisk anxiously, all the mirth and mischief banished from his wee face by this great calamity.

"We must go back at once and find our master," said Nuter the Ryl, who thought and spoke with much deliberation.

"No, no!" exclaimed Peter the Knook, who, cross and crabbed though he was, might always be depended upon in an emergency. "If we delay, or go back, there will not be time to get the toys to the children before morning; and that would grieve Santa Claus more than anything else."

"It is certain that some wicked creatures have captured him," added Kilter thoughtfully, "and their object must be to make the children unhappy. So our first duty is to get the toys distributed as carefully as if Santa Claus were himself present. Afterward we can search for our master and easily secure his freedom."

This seemed such good and sensible advice that the others at once resolved to adopt it. So Peter the Knook called to the reindeer, and the faithful animals again sprang forward and dashed over hill and valley, through forest and plain, until they came to the houses wherein children lay sleeping and dreaming of the pretty gifts they would find on Christmas morning.

The little immortals had set themselves a difficult task; for although they had assisted Santa Claus on many of his journeys, their master had always directed and guided them and told them exactly what he wished them to do. But now they had to distribute the toys according to their own judgment, and they did not understand children as well as did old Santa. So it is no wonder they made some laughable errors.

Mamie Brown, who wanted a doll, got a drum instead; and a drum is of no use to a girl who loves dolls. And Charlie Smith, who delights to romp and play out of doors, and who wanted some new rubber boots to keep his feet dry, received a sewing box filled with colored worsteds and threads and needles, which made him so provoked that he thoughtlessly called our dear Santa Claus a fraud.

Had there been many such mistakes the Daemons would have accomplished their evil purpose and made the children unhappy. But the little friends of the absent Santa Claus labored faithfully and intelligently to carry out their master's ideas, and they made fewer errors than might be expected under such unusual circumstances.

And, although they worked as swiftly as possible, day had begun to break before the toys and other presents were all distributed; so for the first time in many years the reindeer trotted into the Laughing Valley, on their return, in broad daylight, with the brilliant sun peeping over the edge of the forest to prove they were far behind their accustomed hours.

Having put the deer in the stable, the little folk began to wonder how they might rescue their master; and they realized they must discover, first of all, what had happened to him and where he was.

So Wisk the Fairy transported himself to the bower of the Fairy Queen, which was located deep in the heart of the Forest of Burzee; and once there, it did not take him long to find out all about the naughty Daemons and how they had kidnapped the good Santa Claus to prevent his making children happy. The Fairy Queen also promised her assistance, and then, fortified by this powerful support, Wisk flew back to where Nuter and Peter and Kilter awaited him, and the four counseled together and laid plans to rescue their master from his enemies.

It is possible that Santa Claus was not as merry as usual during the night that succeeded his capture. For although he had faith in the judgment of his little friends he could not avoid a certain amount of worry, and an anxious look would creep at times into his kind old eyes as he thought of the disappointment that might await his dear little children. And the Daemons, who guarded him by turns, one after another, did not neglect to taunt him with contemptuous words in his helpless condition.

When Christmas Day dawned the Daemon of Malice was guarding the prisoner, and his tongue was sharper than that of any of the others.

"The children are waking up, Santa!" he cried. "They are waking up to find their stockings empty! Ho, ho! How they will quarrel, and wail, and stamp their feet in anger! Our caves will be full today, old Santa! Our caves are sure to be full!"

But to this, as to other like taunts, Santa Claus answered nothing. He was much grieved by his capture, it is true; but his courage did not forsake him. And, finding that the prisoner would not reply to his jeers, the Daemon of Malice presently went away, and sent the Daemon of Repentance to take his place.

This last personage was not so disagreeable as the others. He had gentle and refined features, and his voice was soft and pleasant in tone.

"My brother Daemons do not trust me overmuch," said he, as he entered the cavern; "but it is morning, now, and the mischief is done. You cannot visit the children again for another year."

"That is true," answered Santa Claus, almost cheerfully; "Christmas Eve is past, and for the first time in centuries I have not visited my children."

"The little ones will be greatly disappointed," murmured the Daemon of Repentance, almost regretfully; "but that cannot be helped now. Their grief is likely to make the children selfish and envious and hateful, and if they come to the Caves of the Daemons today I shall get a chance to lead some of them to my Cave of Repentance."

"Do you never repent, yourself?" asked Santa Claus, curiously.

"Oh, yes, indeed," answered the Daemon. "I am even now repenting that I assisted in your capture. Of course it is too late to remedy the evil that has been done; but repentance, you know, can come only after an evil thought or deed, for in the beginning there is nothing to repent of."

"So I understand," said Santa Claus. "Those who avoid evil need never visit your cave."

"As a rule, that is true," replied the Daemon; "yet you, who have done no evil, are about to visit my cave at once; for to prove that

I sincerely regret my share in your capture I am going to permit you to escape."

This speech greatly surprised the prisoner, until he reflected that it was just what might be expected of the Daemon of Repentance. The fellow at once busied himself untying the knots that bound Santa Claus and unlocking the chains that fastened him to the wall. Then he led the way through a long tunnel until they both emerged in the Cave of Repentance.

"I hope you will forgive me," said the Daemon pleadingly. "I am not really a bad person, you know; and I believe I accomplish a great deal of good in the world."

With this he opened a back door that let in a flood of sunshine, and Santa Claus sniffed the fresh air gratefully.

"I bear no malice," said he to the Daemon, in a gentle voice; "and I am sure the world would be a dreary place without you. So, good morning, and a Merry Christmas to you!"

With these words he stepped out to greet the bright morning, and a moment later he was trudging along, whistling softly to himself, on his way to his home in the Laughing Valley.

Marching over the snow toward the mountain was a vast army, made up of the most curious creatures imaginable. There were numberless knooks from the forest, as rough and crooked in appearance as the gnarled branches of the trees they ministered to. And there were dainty ryls from the fields, each one bearing the emblem of the flower or plant it guarded. Behind these were many ranks of pixies, gnomes and nymphs, and in the rear a thousand beautiful fairies floated along in gorgeous array.

This wonderful army was led by Wisk, Peter, Nuter, and Kilter, who had assembled it to rescue Santa Claus from captivity and to punish the Daemons who had dared to take him away from his beloved children.

And, although they looked so bright and peaceful, the little immortals were armed with powers that would be very terrible to those who had incurred their anger. Woe to the Daemons of the Caves if this mighty army of vengeance ever met them!

But lo! coming to meet his loyal friends appeared the imposing form of Santa Claus, his white beard floating in the breeze and his bright eyes sparkling with pleasure at this proof of the love and veneration he had inspired in the hearts of the most powerful creatures in existence.

And while they clustered around him and danced with glee at his safe return, he gave them earnest thanks for their support. But Wisk, and Nuter, and Peter, and Kilter, he embraced affectionately.

"It is useless to pursue the Daemons," said Santa Claus to the army. "They have their place in the world, and can never be destroyed. But that is a great pity, nevertheless," he continued musingly.

So the fairies, and knooks, and pixies, and ryls all escorted the good man to his castle, and there left him to talk over the events of the night with his little assistants.

Wisk had already rendered himself invisible and flown through the big world to see how the children were getting along on this bright Christmas morning; and by the time he returned, Peter had finished telling Santa Claus of how they had distributed the toys.

"We really did very well," cried the fairy, in a pleased voice; "for I found little unhappiness among the children this morning. Still, you must not get captured again, my dear master; for we might not be so fortunate another time in carrying out your ideas."

He then related the mistakes that had been made, and which he had not discovered until his tour of inspection. And Santa Claus at once sent him with rubber boots for Charlie Smith, and a doll for Mamie Brown; so that even those two disappointed ones became happy.

As for the wicked Daemons of the Caves, they were filled with anger and chagrin when they found that their clever capture of Santa Claus had come to naught. Indeed, no one on that Christmas Day appeared to be at all selfish, or envious, or hateful. And, realizing that while the children's saint had so many powerful friends it was folly to oppose him, the Daemons never again attempted to interfere with his journeys on Christmas Eve.

Christmas Every Day

by William Dean Howells (1892)

The little girl came into her papa's study, as she always did Saturday morning before breakfast, and asked for a story. He tried to beg off that morning, for he was very busy, but she would not let him. So he began:

"Well, once there was a little pig—"

She put her hand over his mouth and stopped him at the word. She said she had heard little pig-stories till she was perfectly sick of them.

"Well, what kind of story *shall* I tell, then?"

"About Christmas. It's getting to be the season. It's past Thanksgiving already."

"It seems to me," her papa argued, "that I've told as often about Christmas as I have about little pigs."

"No difference! Christmas is more interesting."

"Well!" Her papa roused himself from his writing by a great effort. "Well, then, I'll tell you about the little girl that wanted it Christmas every day in the year. How would you like that?"

"First-rate!" said the little girl; and she nestled into comfortable shape in his lap, ready for listening.

"Very well, then, this little pig—Oh, what are you pounding me for?"

"Because you said little pig instead of little girl."

"I should like to know what's the difference between a little pig and a little girl that wanted it Christmas every day!"

"Papa," said the little girl, warningly, "if you don't go on, I'll *give* it to you!" And at this her papa darted off like lightning, and began to tell the story as fast as he could.

Well, once there was a little girl who liked Christmas so much that she wanted it to be Christmas every day in the year; and as soon as Thanksgiving was over she began to send postal-cards to the old Christmas Fairy to ask if she mightn't have it. But the old fairy never answered any of the postals; and after a while the little girl found out that the Fairy was pretty particular, and wouldn't notice anything but letters—not even correspondence cards in envelopes; but real letters on sheets of paper, and sealed outside with a monogram—or your initial, anyway. So, then, she began to send her letters; and in about three weeks—or just the day before Christmas, it was—she got a letter from the Fairy, saying she might have it Christmas every day for a year, and then they would see about having it longer.

The little girl was a good deal excited already, preparing for the old-fashioned, once-a-year Christmas that was coming the next day, and perhaps the Fairy's promise didn't make such an impression on her as it would have made at some other time. She just resolved to keep it to herself, and surprise everybody with it as it kept coming true; and then it slipped out of her mind altogether.

She had a splendid Christmas. She went to bed early, so as to let Santa Claus have a chance at the stockings, and in the morning she was up the first of anybody and went and felt them, and found hers all lumpy with packages of candy, and oranges and grapes, and pocket-books and rubber balls, and all kinds of small presents, and her big brother's with nothing but the tongs in them, and her young lady sister's with a new silk umbrella, and her papa's and mamma's with potatoes and pieces of coal wrapped up in tissue-paper, just as they always had every Christmas. Then she waited around till the rest of the family were up, and she was the first to burst into the library, when the doors were opened, and look at the large presents laid out on the library-table—books, and portfolios, and boxes of stationery, and breastpins, and dolls, and little stoves, and dozens of handkerchiefs, and ink-stands, and skates, and snow-shovels, and photograph-frames, and little easels, and boxes of water-colors, and Turkish paste, and nougat, and candied cherries, and dolls' houses, and waterproofs—and the big Christmas-tree, lighted and standing in a waste-basket in the middle.

She had a splendid Christmas all day. She ate so much candy that she did not want any breakfast; and the whole forenoon the presents kept pouring in that the expressman had not had time to deliver the night before; and she went round giving the presents she had got for other people, and came home and ate[Pg 8] turkey and cranberry for dinner, and plum-pudding and nuts and raisins and oranges and more candy, and then went out and coasted, and came in with a stomach-ache, crying; and her papa said he would see if his house was turned into that sort of fool's paradise another year; and they had a light supper, and pretty early everybody went to bed cross.

Here the little girl pounded her papa in the back, again.

"Well, what now? Did I say pigs?"

"You made them *act* like pigs."

"Well, didn't they?"

"No matter; you oughtn't to put it into a story."

"Very well, then, I'll take it all out."

Her father went on:

The little girl slept very heavily, and she slept very late, but she was wakened at last by the other children dancing[Pg 9] round her bed with their stockings full of presents in their hands.

"What is it?" said the little girl, and she rubbed her eyes and tried to rise up in bed.

"Christmas! Christmas! Christmas!" they all shouted, and waved their stockings.

"Nonsense! It was Christmas yesterday."

Her brothers and sisters just laughed. “We don't know about that. It's Christmas to-day, anyway. You come into the library and see.”

Then all at once it flashed on the little girl that the Fairy was keeping her promise, and her year of Christmases was beginning. She was dreadfully sleepy, but she sprang up like a lark—a lark that had overeaten itself and gone to bed cross—and darted into the library. There it was again! Books, and portfolios, and boxes of stationery, and breastpins—

“You needn't go over it all, papa; I guess I can remember just what was there,” said the little girl.

Well, and there was the Christmas-tree blazing away, and the family picking out their presents, but looking pretty sleepy, and her father perfectly puzzled, and her mother ready to cry. “I'm sure I don't see how I'm to dispose of all these things,” said her mother, and her father said it seemed to him they had had something just like it the day before, but he supposed he must have dreamed it. This struck the little girl as the best kind of a joke; and so she ate so much candy she didn't want any breakfast, and went round carrying presents, and had turkey and cranberry for dinner, and then went out and coasted, and came in with a—

“Papa!”

“Well, what now?”

“What did you promise, you forgetful thing?”

“Oh! oh yes!”

Well, the next day, it was just the same thing over again, but everybody getting crosser; and at the end of a week's time so many people had lost their tempers that you could pick up lost tempers anywhere; they perfectly strewed the ground. Even when people tried to recover their tempers they usually got somebody else's, and it made the most dreadful mix.

The little girl began to get frightened, keeping the secret all to herself; she wanted to tell her mother, but she didn't dare to; and she was ashamed to ask the Fairy to take back her gift, it seemed ungrateful and ill-bred, and she thought she would try to stand it, but she hardly knew how she could, for a whole year. So it went on and on, and it was Christmas on St. Valentine's Day and Washington's Birthday, just the same as any day, and it didn't skip even the First of April, though everything was counterfeit that day, and that was some *little* relief.

After a while coal and potatoes began to be awfully scarce, so many had been wrapped up in tissue-paper to fool papas and mammas with. Turkeys got to be about a thousand dollars apiece—

"Papa!"

"Well, what?"

"You're beginning to fib."

"Well, *two* thousand, then."

And they got to passing off almost anything for turkeys—half-grown humming-birds, and even rocs out of the *Arabian Nights*—the real turkeys were so scarce. And cranberries—well, they asked a diamond apiece for cranberries.

All the woods and orchards were cut down for Christmas-trees, and where[Pg 13] the woods and orchards used to be it looked just like a stubble-field, with the stumps. After a while they had to make Christmas-trees out of rags, and stuff them with bran, like old-fashioned dolls; but there were plenty of rags, because people got so poor, buying presents for one another, that they couldn't get any new clothes, and they just wore their old ones to tatters. They got so poor that everybody had to go to the poor-house, except the confectioners, and the fancy-store keepers, and the picture-book sellers, and the expressmen; and *they* all got so rich and proud that they would hardly wait upon a person when he came to buy. It was perfectly shameful!

Well, after it had gone on about three or four months, the little girl, whenever she came into the room in the morning and saw those great ugly, lumpy stockings dangling at the fire-place, and the disgusting presents around everywhere, used to just sit down and burst out crying. In six months she was perfectly exhausted; she couldn't even cry any more; she just lay on the lounge and rolled her eyes and panted. About the beginning of October she took to sitting down on dolls wherever she found them—French dolls, or any kind—she hated the sight of them so; and by Thanksgiving she was crazy, and just slammed her presents across the room.

By that time people didn't carry presents around nicely any more. They flung them over the fence, or through the window, or anything; and, instead of running their tongues out and taking great pains to write "For dear Papa," or "Mamma," or "Brother," or "Sister," or "Susie," or "Sammie," or "Billie," or "Bobbie," or "Jimmie," or "Jennie," or whoever it was, and troubling to get the spelling right, and then signing their names, and "Xmas, 18—," they used to write in the gift-books, "Take it, you horrid old thing!" and then go and bang it against the front door. Nearly everybody had built barns to hold their presents, but pretty soon the barns overflowed, and then they used to let them lie out in the rain, or anywhere. Sometimes the police used to come and tell them to shovel their presents off the sidewalk, or they would arrest them.

"I thought you said everybody had gone to the poor-house," interrupted the little girl.

"They did go, at first," said her papa; "but after a while the poor-houses got so full that they had to send the people back to their own houses. They tried to cry, when they got back, but they couldn't make the least sound."

"Why couldn't they?"

"Because they had lost their voices, saying 'Merry Christmas' so much. Did I tell you how it was on the Fourth of July?"

"No; how was it?" And the little girl nestled closer, in expectation of something uncommon.

Well, the night before, the boys stayed up to celebrate, as they always do, and fell asleep before twelve o'clock, as usual, expecting to be wakened by the bells and cannon. But it was nearly eight o'clock before the first boy in the United States woke up, and then he found out what the trouble was. As soon as he could get his clothes on he ran out of the house and smashed a big cannon-torpedo down on the pavement; but it didn't make any more noise than a damp wad of paper; and after he tried about twenty or thirty more, he began to pick them up and look at them. Every single torpedo was a big raisin!

Then he just streaked it up-stairs, and examined his fire-crackers and toy-pistol and two-dollar collection of fireworks, and found that they were nothing but sugar and candy painted up to look like fireworks! Before ten o'clock every boy in the United States found out that his Fourth of July things had turned into Christmas things; and then they just sat down and cried—they were so mad. There are about twenty million boys in the United States, and so you can imagine what a noise they made. Some men got together before night, with a little powder that hadn't turned into purple sugar yet, and they said they would fire off *one* cannon, anyway. But the cannon burst into a thousand pieces, for it was nothing but rock-candy, and some of the men nearly got killed. The Fourth of July orations all turned into Christmas carols, and when anybody tried to read the Declaration, instead of saying, "When in the course of human events it becomes necessary," he was sure to sing, "God rest you, merry gentlemen." It was perfectly awful.

The little girl drew a deep sigh of satisfaction.

"And how was it at Thanksgiving?"

Her papa hesitated. "Well, I'm almost afraid to tell you. I'm afraid you'll think it's wicked."

"Well, tell, anyway," said the little girl.

Well, before it came Thanksgiving it had leaked out who had caused all these Christmases. The little girl had suffered so much that she had talked about it in her sleep; and after that hardly anybody would play with her. People just perfectly despised her, because if it had not been for her greediness it wouldn't have happened; and now, when it came Thanksgiving, and she wanted them to go to church, and have squash-pie and turkey, and show their gratitude, they said that all the turkeys had been eaten up for her old Christmas dinners, and if she would stop the Christmases, they would see about the gratitude. Wasn't it dreadful? And the very next day the little girl began to send letters to the Christmas Fairy, and then telegrams, to stop it. But it didn't do any good; and then she got to calling at the Fairy's house, but the girl that came to the door always said, "Not at home," or "Engaged," or "At dinner," or something like that; and so it went on till it came to the old once-a-year Christmas Eve. The little girl fell asleep, and when she woke up in the morning—

"She found it was all nothing but a dream," suggested the little girl.

"No, indeed!" said her papa. "It was all every bit true!"

"Well, what *did* she find out, then?"

"Why, that it wasn't Christmas at last, and wasn't ever going to be, any more. Now it's time for breakfast."

The little girl held her papa fast around the neck.

"You sha'n't go if you're going to leave it *so*!"

"How do you want it left?"

"Christmas once a year."

"All right," said her papa; and he went on again.

Well, there was the greatest rejoicing all over the country, and it extended clear up into Canada. The people met together everywhere, and kissed and cried for joy. The city carts went around and gathered up all the candy and raisins and nuts, and dumped them into the river; and it made the fish perfectly sick; and the whole United States, as far out as Alaska, was one blaze of bonfires, where the children were burning up their gift-books and presents of all kinds. They had the greatest *time*!

The little girl went to thank the old Fairy because she had stopped its being Christmas, and she said she hoped she would keep her promise and see that Christmas never, never came again. Then the Fairy frowned, and asked her if she was sure she knew what she meant; and the little girl asked her, Why not? and the old Fairy said that now she was behaving just as greedily as ever, and she'd better look out. This made the little girl think it all over carefully again, and she said she would be willing to have it Christmas about once in a thousand years; and then she said a hundred, and then she said ten, and at last she got down to one. Then the Fairy said that was the good old way that had pleased people ever since Christmas began, and she was agreed. Then the little girl said, “What're your shoes made of?” And the Fairy said, “Leather.” And the little girl said, “Bargain's done forever,” and skipped off, and hippity-hopped the whole way home, she was so glad.

“How will that do?” asked the papa.

“First-rate!” said the little girl; but she hated to have the story stop, and was rather sober. However, her mamma put her head in at the door, and asked her papa:

“Are you never coming to breakfast? What have you been telling that child?”

“Oh, just a moral tale.”

The little girl caught him around the neck again.

"*We* know! Don't you tell *what*, papa! Don't you tell *what*!"

Author Biographies

Our authors –

Louisa May Alcott (1832–1888)

An American novelist and poet best known for her novel *Little Women* and its sequels. She wrote under several pen names and often tackled themes of domestic life, moral development, and women's independence.

L. Frank Baum (1856–1919)

An American author best known for writing *The Wonderful Wizard of Oz* and its sequels. His imaginative stories have become enduring classics in American children's literature.

Willa Cather (1873–1947)

An American author known for her novels about frontier life on the Great Plains, such as *My Ántonia* and *O Pioneers*! Her works explore themes of identity, hardship, and the American experience.

Francis P. Church (1839–1906)

An American editor and writer, best known for his editorial 'Yes, Virginia, there is a Santa Claus,' published in *The New York Sun* in 1897. The piece has become one of the most famous editorials ever written.

Elizabeth Harrison (1849–1927)

An American educator and author who advocated for early childhood education. She founded what became the National College of Education and wrote many stories that reflected moral and educational themes.

O. Henry (1862–1910)

Born William Sydney Porter, an American short story writer known for his wit, wordplay, and twist endings. His most famous stories include 'The Gift of the Magi' and 'The Ransom of Red Chief.'

William Dean Howells (1837–1920)

An American realist author and literary critic, often called 'The Dean of American Letters.' He supported authors like Mark Twain and Henry James and wrote novels such as *The Rise of Silas Lapham*.

Clement Clarke Moore (1779–1863)

An American scholar and poet, famously credited with writing 'A Visit from St. Nicholas' (also known as 'Twas the Night Before Christmas'), a poem that helped shape the modern image of Santa Claus.

Booth Tarkington (1869–1946)

An American novelist and dramatist best known for his novels about the American Midwest. He won the Pulitzer Prize for Fiction twice and is remembered for works like *The Magnificent Ambersons* and *Penrod*.

Henry Van Dyke (1852–1933)

An American author, educator, and clergyman. He is known for his inspirational writings, including 'The Other Wise Man' and 'The First Christmas Tree.'

www.ingramcontent.com/pod-product-compliance
Lightning Source LLC
Chambersburg PA
CBHW010358310726
48979CB00006B/1080

* 9 7 8 1 9 9 8 6 3 0 6 0 8 *